WINNING BIG ...

a little love story for all ages

by
Judith Keim

Wild Quail Publishing

This is a work of fiction. Names, characters, places, public or private institutions, corporations, towns, and incidents are the product of the author's imagination or are used fictitiously. Any resemblance to actual events, locales, or persons, living or dead, is coincidental.

No part of this book may be reproduced or transmitted in any form or by any electronic or mechanical means, including information storage and retrieval systems, without permission in writing from the author, except by a reviewer, who may quote brief passages in a review. This book may not be resold or uploaded for distribution to others.

Wild Quail Publishing
PO Box 171332
Boise, ID 83717-1332

ISBN# 978-0-9964350-9-3

Dedication

This author believes love is essential for all creatures, big and small, and that true love fulfills us and comforts us in a way unlike any other. The story told here is to be shared with others of all sizes, shapes, colors and backgrounds in the hopes that they, too, find happiness and love.

Foreword

Hotels are fascinating places. Interesting people come and go, and a variety of hotel staff members assist them with a number of happy occasions. For a writer, it is a place of stories—real and imagined. My husband's entire career has been associated with hotels. At the time this story was written, my husband and I and our dachshund, Winston, were living at a seaside resort for two years while he worked on a project there.

As famous people and others came and went, I watched them and made up stories about them, as all writers are wont to do. And then, for fun, I imagined what it would be like if a whole different group—a population of mice—existed behind the hotel walls. No respectable hotel would permit this, of course, which made it even more fun to write about it. I imagined what their lives might be like. Surely they would know love, mystery, and excitement like human guests. And so it began ...

Here is Theodore and Lila's story—a celebration of romance and happy endings.

Early readers have said of it: "Every kind of delight;" "Charming;" "The perfect little gift for the holidays and special occasions;" "A book that really does win big!"

Enjoy!

CHAPTER ONE

Standing beside the entrance to the glitzy beachside hotel in Florida, Theodore straightened his coat, doffed his hat, and took a deep bow. "Welcome to The Winston, sir."

The man's huge brown shoes marched by Theodore's furry body without missing a step. Theodore shot a disappointed look at his grandfather, who nodded his gray mouse head.

"It's all right, son. This hotel is as much ours as anyone else's, and you did the right thing by greeting him properly. That's what I've been doing for years. Now, it's your turn."

Theodore ran a paw over his whiskers and took a deep breath. It was an honor to be selected as the doorman representing the mice in the building. The demanding, human guests arriving here weren't always aware of the smaller guests accompanying them, but each needed to be given a suitable welcome.

It was true, though, that if any mouse was ever discovered in the people's part of the hotel, they would all be eliminated.

That was a scary thought for Theodore, who had to do his job discreetly.

A white, stretch limo pulled up to the hotel's entrance.

"Here she comes. Zanna Loverly," prompted Grandfather. "She deserves extra-special attention, not only as a movie star, but because she's such a nice human."

A short, curvy woman with long, blond hair stepped out of the car and waved to everyone. Her bright-red lips curved pleasantly as people stopped what they were doing and stared. A young girl rushed over to her and asked for an autograph. Zanna cheerfully complied before she turned and walked toward the front door.

Theodore doffed his hat and took a deep bow. "Welcome to The Winston, Ma'am."

Grandfather coughed and shook his head. "Never call a movie star Ma'am, no matter how old she is. They like Miss much better."

In awe, Theodore stared up, up, up at the well-known starlet's face. As she strode inside, Zanna's silver heels tapped the entrance's marble floor in a loud staccato. The sweet smell of flowers followed her.

Grandfather nudged Theodore. "Here comes the one I've been waiting for. Her name is Lila. She goes everywhere with Zanna. "

Theodore straightened, prepared to bow.

A white mouse wearing a pink boa and a sparkly pink dress jumped out of the limousine, scampered toward the bushes, then sashayed toward the mouse's entrance.

"Welcome to The Winston," said Theodore, mesmerized by the prettiest mouse he'd ever seen. Her eyes were the palest pink, her tiny nose a shade darker. She arched her tail in a perky pose and stopped, looking him over ever so closely.

"I-I hope you have a lovely stay," stammered Theodore. "Let me know if there's anything I can do for you. Anything at all."

"Humph." Her nostrils flared the tiniest bit. She lifted her nose. Without a backward glance, she walked behind the bushes alongside the hotel's main entrance and into the special revolving door for mice. Theodore watched as she kept pace with the door's circular movement by doing a delicate tip-toed dance.

"Ahhh," sighed Theodore. His heart pounded in his chest. She was ... lovely, he thought, caressing the word in his mind.

"Never, never, do that," grumped Grandfather, jarring Theodore out of his trance. "You acted like you wanted to date her. She's a guest. You're just the doorman. Understand?" He glared at Theodore. "Now get that dreamy expression off your face."

Theodore blinked. "But she's the most beautiful mouse I've ever seen."

Grandfather shook a paw at him. "There are a lot of beautiful creatures here at The Winston. You're going to see many of them. However, a good doorman remembers his place and is always a gentleman." He stopped talking as several pairs of scruffy sneakers raced by.

"Wel ..." Before Theodore could squeak out the rest of his greeting, the sneakers disappeared from view with several noisy slaps on the pavement.

"Don't worry about them." Grandfather clapped Theodore's shoulder. "They're kids out of control and without any manners." He let out a laugh that wasn't altogether merry. "Oh, yes. Your life is about to change forever with this job."

Theodore's brow creased with worry. No matter how hard the work was, he had to succeed. After his father's untimely death, he was in charge of the family. His mother was counting on him to provide a safe place for her and his thirteen siblings and to make sure they had plenty to eat. Working as the doorman at The Winston would ensure that.

A long, black limousine glided up to the front entrance. The driver stopped the car, got out, and ran around to the back door, which he opened with a flourish.

Waiting to see who would appear, Theodore held his breath.

Long tan legs above a pair of red, spike-heeled shoes emerged from the limo. The dark-haired woman who stepped onto the sidewalk was as beautiful as Zanna Loverly, but a frown marred her brow. When someone started to approach her, she waved them away.

A small, white, fluffy dog leaped out of the car, looked around and yapped.

"The dog! Get the dog!" the glamorous woman ordered the driver. "Here, Fifi!"

The dog ignored her mistress and headed right for Theodore, a murderous look in her eye.

Theodore froze with shock.

Grandfather grabbed Theodore's arm and jerked him inside the mouse entrance. From behind the glass of the tiny revolving door, Theodore shrank from the dog's ferocious scowl as she showed her teeth and barked.

The driver picked up the dog and handed her over to her mistress. Safe for the moment, Theodore's body still trembled as he observed the woman rain a number of kisses on the dangerous little dog.

Beside him, Grandfather clucked his tongue. "Pampered dogs like that can be a nuisance. We must be alert to them."

"Who is that lady?"

Grandfather's lip curled. "Simone Skinner. She's Zanna Loverly's arch enemy. I wonder why they're here together. It can't be good."

Another black limousine pulled up out front. Theodore checked to make sure the dog was safely in the lobby before hurrying outside to ensure any small guests would be properly greeted.

Two gentlemen exited the car. One was a short, heavy-set man whose gray hair formed a long, curly fringe around his head. The other was a movie star Theodore recognized. With his muscular body, bad boy reputation, and easy smile, Rocky Strong was everyone's favorite hero. Theodore's mother was a big fan.

"Who's the guy with Rocky?" Theodore asked.

Grandfather shook his head with disgust. "A big-wig producer by the name of Samuel Horner. He comes here quite often. He's a real cheapskate. Word is he doesn't leave the maid a tip, and whenever he eats in his fancy suite, he doesn't leave any scraps for the rest of us."

The driver and the bellman struggled with luggage as the men headed indoors. During the commotion, a gray mouse wearing a bright red bandana around his head swaggered toward the mouse entrance of the hotel.

Theodore gave his grandfather a questioning look.

"His name's Bandit. He travels with Rocky."

"Yo! How's it going?" Bandit said, holding up a fist to be bumped.

Not sure how to respond, Theodore doffed his hat. "Welcome to The Winston."

Bandit blinked. "Huh? Are you for real?"

Theodore pulled himself up as tall as he could, but he was no match for Bandit's height. "I'm the new doorman. I'm just doing my job."

"Well, little guy. I best go inside. I understand Lila is here."

Theodore could feel the blood leave his furry face. Was Bandit Lila's boyfriend?

Grandfather nudged him. "Here's another one."

A mouse as wide as he was tall approached, munching on a piece of particularly rotten cheese.

"Maurice. Mr. Horner's traveling companion," prompted Grandfather.

"Welcome to The Winston," Theodore said, forgetting to doff his hat as he stared at Maurice's round stomach. Too busy munching on his cheese to acknowledge Theodore, the mouse named Maurice made his way inside the hotel.

"No matter how rude our esteemed guests may behave," said Grandfather, "the doorman never expresses his disapproval."

Theodore nodded. He was discovering that being a

doorman at a fancy hotel was no easy task. He spent the rest of the morning bowing and greeting guests of all shapes, sizes, and types.

When another limousine pulled up to the front entrance, the woman inside stepped onto the pavement before the doorman could reach the car door to help her. She stood there, cigarette in hand, tapping the toe of her strappy shoe against the cement beneath her feet.

"Well, where is he?" she said in a loud, grating voice. She pushed her sunglasses atop her bleached hair and glanced around impatiently.

Mr. Horner rushed through the front doorway. "Juliet, my dear. So glad you could make it. I think you're going to be happy you came here."

"I'd better be," she warned him. "I didn't make this trip just to please *you*."

Listening to this exchange, Theodore was very sure he wouldn't call this starlet Ma'am. She wouldn't like it at all.

As Juliet and Mr. Horner entered the hotel, Theodore turned to see a brown mouse race toward him, carrying a bunch of notebooks. Behind her big, round glasses, her eyes glared at him.

"Can't you see I need help?" she said.

Theodore's welcome stuck inside his throat. He hurried to her side. "I'll get a bellman to help you with your things."

"Yes, that would be a good idea," she snapped. "So glad you thought of it."

Theodore found someone inside to help with the new guest's belongings and, shaking his head at the way she was scolding the bellman, he returned to his post. Since coming to live and work at The Winston Hotel, he'd quickly learned all kinds of guests came there. Some easy. Some not.

By noon, Theodore was exhausted from smiling, nodding,

bowing, and greeting the guests.

Grandfather gave him a pat on the back. "You can go to lunch now. I'll take over."

His stomach growling with hunger, Theodore hurried through the mouse's entrance into the hotel. Following a carefully planned trail through the structure of the building, he made his way to the mice's cafeteria. Since no mice were ever allowed in the people's part of the hotel, they had established a hotel of their own behind the interior walls of the building.

Located behind the hotel's kitchen, the cafeteria served a whole variety of mice workers—maids, engineers, office staff, security people, even wait staff. Sitting in a cordoned-off area away from the staff, the small guests of the hotel ate there as well. Unlike the tables and benches in the staff area, hotel mouse guests sat at tables covered in crisp white linen. Candles placed next to colorful flowers in crystal vases flickered atop the round tables. Staff and guests were able to watch the chef and his team work behind a glass partition lining one wall of the cafeteria as they prepared bits and pieces of food that had been gathered.

Theodore took his place in the food line and stared at the juicy, colorful remnants of a beach party the hotel staff had thrown for their guests last night. His mouth watered. By the looks of it, the party had been quite an affair—pieces of cheese, shrimp, beef, chicken, and various side dishes were spread out alongside leafy leftovers from salad. He could hardly wait to dig in.

The squeaks and murmurings in the cafeteria suddenly stopped.

"There she is," someone said in a hushed voice.

Lila swished into the room, all but dancing on her toes as she made her way to the back corner.

Theodore's heart pounded. Though he knew he shouldn't, he lifted a paw and waved at her.

She glanced at him and turned away, then took a seat at a table for two.

Bandit appeared next. The digits or "fingers" of his paw formed a V as he waved to the crowd, every much a hero as Rocky Strong. He strolled over to Lila's table and took a seat opposite her.

Watching from a distance, Theodore's stomach churned. He'd been so proud to be the new doorman, but now he realized it wasn't good enough. Not for Lila.

"Hello, son!"

Theodore forgot all about impressing Lila as he turned to face his mother. She was the reason he'd fought hard for the job of doorman. With too many children to care for on her own, she couldn't manage without his help.

His mother's lips spread into a wide smile. She gave him a quick hug. "You look so handsome in that uniform. I'm proud of you, Theodore."

Theodore nodded absently. His gaze swung to the table in the corner. Lila and Bandit were laughing over something she'd said.

His mother noticed him watching Lila and frowned. "Don't be thinking foolish things. You'll only get hurt."

Theodore sighed and tugged at the collar of the uniform he'd once thought so wonderful. Somehow he'd earn Lila's admiration. He just didn't know how.

CHAPTER TWO

Lying in bed that night, Theodore thought back to his first day on the job. Grandfather had said working at the hotel would change his life. It already had. Seeing one little white mouse called Lila had added a new dimension to what he now thought of as a boring existence.

One of his little brothers crept up to him. "Can I come into bed with you, Theodore? I had one of my bad dreams."

Theodore nodded. "Sure. I'll keep you safe." After his father's horrible death in the alley outside the hotel, he'd had to put aside all dreams for himself. His family needed him now.

"Will you tell me a story?"

Theodore looked down at his brother. "Sure. One time, a beautiful white mouse came to the hotel. She was like a princess. Know what I mean?"

The little mousekin nodded.

Theodore was so busy telling a tale about a hero just like him who saved that beautiful mouse from a very big, very dangerous cat that he didn't realize his brother was already fast asleep.

When Theodore awoke the next morning, he discovered not one brother, but two mousekins huddled beside him. Careful not to wake them, Theodore climbed out of bed and got dressed. He checked the clock on the wall. He'd have just enough time to go to the cafeteria, grab a bite to eat, and bring food to his mother, brothers, and sisters before beginning another day as doorman.

The sun had barely risen in the sky when Theodore

hurried into the employees' cafeteria. At the sound of quiet sobbing, Theodore turned. Lila was sitting at a table in the corner all alone, her face in her paws, her shoulders shaking.

Theodore's heart clenched. He rushed over to her. "Lila! I mean, Miss ... I mean Miss Lila, are you all right?"

Lila looked up at him. Her pink eyes flooded with tears. "It's Zanna. She and Simone had a terrible fight, all because of the movie Mr. Horner, the producer, is making with Rocky Strong. Simone found out Zanna might get the role opposite Rocky, and she stormed into Zanna's hotel room. The two of them shrieked and fought like ... like ... cats! I wanted to help Zanna, I really did, but I could only watch what was going on because Fifi was there."

"Is Zanna okay?" Theodore couldn't hide his alarm. It couldn't have been a fair fight. Zanna was much smaller than Simone.

Lila shrugged. "I don't know. That awful dog chased me out of the room." She clasped her paws together. "I was so afraid one of the humans would see me. I'd never forgive myself if all the mice were thrown out of here because of me."

Theodore nodded. All their guests knew mice were not permitted in the humans' part of the hotel. It was one of the hotel's strictest rules. "So what happened next?"

"When I went back to check on her, Zanna had a black eye and she was asleep." Fresh tears rolled down Lila's white, furry face. "I should have done something to help her."

"I'm sure she'll be fine." Theodore fought to keep his voice calm. Being this close to Lila made his heart race so fast he thought he'd faint.

Lila blotted her eyes with a tiny, lace handkerchief. "I've been with Zanna since she was a girl. I feel terrible. You know how it is when you feel responsible for someone?"

"I know." Theodore thought of his brothers and sisters. As much as he wanted to stay with Lila, he couldn't. "Look, I've got to go take care of my family. Let me know if you need any help."

She let out a shaky sigh and waved goodbye.

Theodore grabbed as much food as his paws could hold and hurried out of the room.

After quickly dividing up the food among his siblings, he rushed to the front entrance of the hotel. His grandfather was standing at the doorman's station, checking his watch. "I thought you were going to be late, Theodore. We can't have that, can we?"

"No, sir," said Theodore, catching his breath. It was going to be a long morning. He hadn't had time to eat, and already a pair of big brown loafers was headed his way. He doffed his hat and bowed.

"Good morning, sir. Welcome to The Winston."

The loafers marched on by, followed by an old female mouse, walking with a cane. Theodore rushed over to her and helped her inside.

When another set of shoes, black slip-ons, followed by a spry, young mouse exited the hotel, Theodore bobbed his head. "Have a good day, and be sure to come back and visit us."

Smiling, the mouse waved goodbye.

Grandfather gave Theodore a nod of approval. "Keep up the good work. I'm going to go to breakfast. Remember, a doorman never leaves his post unattended. See you later."

A number of people and smaller guests arrived at or left the hotel in a steady stream. Theodore had lost count of just how many when he heard a sweet, high voice call his name. He turned to see Lila by the mouse entrance waving frantically to him.

"Come quickly! I need your help!"

He paused. Grandfather's words came to him. *A doorman never leaves his post unattended.*

"Theodore, I need you!" Lila's words were like woven, golden threads, drawing him toward her.

"What's wrong?"

Lila's eyes filled. "It's Zanna. I'm worried about her. I tried to wake her up, but she didn't move— not even when I tried to shake her shoulder. It's way past time for her morning exercise. Something's wrong. I know it."

"What do you want me to do?" Theodore's paws itched to wipe the tears from her sweet face.

"You have to come with me. We need to get her some help."

Maybe Zanna was dying, thought Theodore with dismay. That would be awful, and bad for the hotel. He glanced around, then followed Lila inside. He had to make it quick or he might lose his job. "Which room is Zanna in?"

"2404," said Lila, starting to run.

Theodore followed her up through the plumbing system behind the interior walls of the hotel, careful to avoid the pipes that were hot.

"Here we are," said Lila, coming to a stop. She entered a hole, pushed open a small piece of baseboard, and crawled through. Theodore followed, entering the dim interior of a closet stuffed with clothes and shoes.

Lila waved him forward. "Hurry!"

Theodore scampered out of the closet into the largest, fanciest bedroom he'd ever seen—a luxurious room no hotel would ever want a mouse to see.

Lila nudged him. "She's up there!"

Theodore scooted up onto the wide, king-sized bed and stared at the woman who'd been so cheerful the day before.

She lay sprawled across the sheets, her eyes closed, her mouth hanging open. A black bruise circled one eye.

Lila crept up to Zanna and tugged on her earlobe. "Time to get up," she squeaked.

Zanna didn't move.

A suspicion crossed Theodore's mind. He went over to the empty glass lying on the bedside table and took a sniff. "I think I know what the problem is. This smells weird. Zanna must have taken sleeping medication of some kind."

Lila shook her head back and forth so hard her diamond earrings flashed. "Zanna never does anything like that. Medication of any kind makes her sick. She always says drugs are bad for her." She took a whiff of the glass's interior. "Ugh! This smells like alcohol, and she doesn't drink that stuff." She turned to Theodore wide-eyed. "Maybe somebody tried to kill her."

"We have to get someone up here right away," said Theodore, suddenly afraid for Zanna's life.

Lila clasped her paws with worry. "How are we going to do that?"

"I'll call the front desk," Theodore answered with bravado, not certain he could pull it off. He tried to push the receiver off the phone. It barely moved.

"Here, I'll help," said Lila.

Together, they pushed and shoved until the receiver fell to the table with a thud that would have awakened a person sleeping normally.

"Now what," said Lila, gazing at Zanna with concern. "Hurry! She's looking funny."

Theodore crawled up onto the numbers pad and read the list of extensions. "It says Front Desk-4. Here goes." He jumped on # 4 as hard as he could.

"Hello, this is The Winston Hotel. It's my pleasure to serve you. How may I help you?"

Theodore gave Lila an encouraging smile.

"Hello? Hello?"

The right words came to Theodore's mind, but all he could say was, "Squeak!"

"Hello? Hello?" The desk clerk hung up the phone with a loud click that hurt Theodore's ears.

"Oh, no!" cried Lila. "Now, what are we going to do?"

Theodore cut off the call and jumped up and down on the #4 button.

"Hello, this is the Winston Hotel. It's my pleasure to serve you. How may I help you?"

"Squeak!" shouted Theodore.

"Hello? Hello?"

Theodore took a big breath. "SQUEEEEAK!"

"Look, I don't know what you want, but I'll go ahead and send someone right up."

Lila ran over to Theodore and threw her arms around him. "You did it! Thank you!"

Theodore's knees went weak. If he lived to be one hundred, he'd always remember this moment, this wonderful feeling of Lila hugging him.

Lila let go of him, raced over to Zanna, and took hold of one of her fingers. "Hang on! Help is on the way!"

A knock sounded at the door.

"C'mon!" Theodore waved to Lila to follow him. "We've got to get out of here."

Lila shook her head. "I can't leave until I know she's okay."

The door opened.

Theodore grabbed Lila's paw and dragged her off the bed.

A maid stood in the doorway, wide-eyed. "Eeeek!"

"What's wrong?" said a voice behind the maid—a voice Theodore recognized as Simone's.

The maid pointed into the room to the bed. "There! A body on the bed!"

"No, Fifi!" shrieked Simone. But the dog jumped out of her arms and charged inside, heading right for Theodore and Lila.

Theodore kept hold of Lila's paw and scurried as fast as he could toward the window. They'd just reached the drapes lining the window when the dog lunged at them. Shaking, they hid behind the heavy material.

"Fifi, come here!" Simon shouted.

Fifi's black nose appeared behind the drape, followed by a mouthful of teeth. The dog growled and snapped at Lila, barely missing her.

"Up! We have to go up." Theodore gave Lila a push onto the fabric. He followed behind, trying to ignore the dog's sharp white teeth snapping at his tail.

Out of the dog's reach, Theodore clung to the fabric next to Lila and strained to hear what was going on in the room.

"Zanna!" cried Simone. "Wake up!"

"What's going on here?" asked a male voice. "We've been getting strange phone calls from this room."

"It's her. I can't wake her up," said Simone.

"I'm calling 911 now," said the man. "Whose dog is that? Keep it quiet while I talk!"

"Fifi, come here," said Simone.

The dog stood still, looking up at Theodore and Lila with hungry eyes.

"I'm slipping on this shiny fabric," whispered Lila, giving Theodore a panicky look.

"Me, too," he said, gripping the fabric as hard as he could. "Is there another way out of the room?"

"I don't think so," said Lila. "The only entrance I found was the hole in the closet."

Fifi charged the drapes, shaking them furiously.

"Help!" squeaked Lila. She held out a paw and Theodore grabbed it. But with the addition of her weight, he knew it wouldn't be long before he fell to the floor.

"Get the dog out of here," ordered the male voice. "The ambulance attendants are on their way."

"Shouldn't I stay to make sure she's all right?" said Simone.

"Are you a friend of hers?" asked the man.

"Not really," Simone said.

"Say ... aren't you one of the movie stars staying here?"

"Me?" said Simone. "No. You must be thinking of someone else. I'd better take the dog and go."

Theodore watched Fifi being dragged away from the window. He let out a sigh of relief that the dog was gone. Then he frowned. Why was Simone lying about being a movie star? Was she up to something rotten?

CHAPTER THREE

The emergency team arrived in Zanna's room with a gurney. Peeking out from behind the drapes, Theodore silently cheered. While everyone's attention was on Zanna, he and Lila made a mad dash for the closet, staying close to the edge of the room. He had to get back to his post before anyone noticed he was missing.

Lila stopped him in the closet. "You go on ahead. I'm going to hide in here until I know Zanna is okay. Thank you so much for your help." Her eyes shone. She lifted to her toes and planted a quick kiss on his cheek. "I couldn't have done this on my own."

Theodore lifted a paw to his face. Feeling as if he were in a dream, he could think of nothing extraordinary to say. He doffed his cap and bowed. "At your service, Miss Lila."

"Better hurry back to your post, Doorman," she said, shattering the idea in Theodore's mind that he was more than that to her. His spirits plummeted.

Aware of the time, he raced down through the maze of pipes and rushed outside.

From Theodore's post, Grandfather glared at him. "Where were you?"

Theodore gulped. "I was helping one of our guests."

"Does this have anything to do with Lila and Zanna?"

Theodore blinked in surprise. "How did ..."

Grandfather cut him off. "Nothing is secret among the staff in a hotel. And that includes the fact you have disobeyed orders, which is why you are now fired from your job."

"Fired?" Theodore's stomach sank to his feet. "But what

about my mother and my brothers and sisters? They need me to do my job."

Grandfather wagged a paw at him. "You should have thought of that before you left your post."

The clack of high heels against the pavement cut short their conversation.

Theodore doffed his hat and bowed. "Welcome to The Winston, Miss. We hope you enjoy your stay."

"Hold on." Grandfather put a hand on Theodore's shoulder.

Theodore turned to him. "Please, Grandfather, give me another chance. I can't disappoint the rest of the family."

Grandfather stared at him for so long Theodore nervously twitched his whiskers.

"All right," sighed Grandfather. "One more chance. But from now on you have to be more responsible. I covered for you this time, but I won't do it again. Understand?"

Theodore nodded. What he'd thought had been a dream come true with Lila kissing him was turning into a nightmare that wasn't about to go away.

A pair of flip flops was leaving the scene. "Good day, sir. We hope you had a pleasant stay. Please come back and visit us again," Theodore said.

"Good boy," said Grandfather, and left Theodore alone to do his job.

The cafeteria was filled with noisy, excited squeaks. Theodore glanced at the table in the corner. A crowd had gathered around Lila. He paused, hoping she'd notice him, but she was too busy talking to Bandit and the other important guests.

"Hi, Theodore," said one of his younger sisters. She came

up to him and took his paw. "Come sit with us."

"I'll be right there." He picked up a tray and surveyed the food laid out in an attractive arrangement. By the looks of it, one of the groups "in house" must have had a fancy breakfast. His stomach growled. He loved cheese omelets and sweet rolls, especially when Henrique, the mice's chef, added his own extra touches—grated Swiss cheese for the omelets and cinnamon sugar on the rolls.

As he carried his tray over to his family's table, he saw Maurice sitting by himself behind a mountain of food. Maurice stopped eating when he noticed Theodore looking at him, then turned his gaze away and dug into his food.

"Come have a seat," urged Theodore's mother.

Theodore shot another glance at Lila's corner table and sat down. Soon his attention was diverted by all the talk at the table. Listening to his younger brothers and sisters tell him about their new teacher, he smiled. He well remembered his own classroom scenes.

"We learnt all about cats," said one of his brothers, round-eyed. "We have to be careful with them. They could ..." he gulped nervously ... "they could *eat* us!"

"Don't forget about dogs," said Theodore. He'd been frightened silly when Fifi had chased Lila and him.

"The dog lesson comes next week," his brother said, proudly.

Theodore shook a paw at him. "Well, this week you'd better remember there's a dog in the hotel. Be careful."

"Listen to your big brother," warned Theodore's mother.

Theodore returned her smile but couldn't help glancing at the table in the corner. Lila and Bandit were alone now, and he was holding her paw.

Theodore's mother gave him a worried look and rose from her seat. "You're just the doorman. Remember?" She walked away, trailed by his brothers and sisters.

Alone, Theodore pushed away his food. Seeing how Lila was with Bandit, he was too sad to take another bite.

"So, you're a hero or something?"

The bossy mouse who'd accompanied Juliet appeared beside Theodore's table. She took a seat opposite him and stared at him from behind her big, round glasses.

"So what's the problem with Zanna? Another one of her dramatic scenes?"

"What do you mean?" Theodore didn't like her or the tone of her voice.

The mouse's lip curled. "Juliet says she's a drama queen. That's all. So, what happened?" She leaned forward, greedy for details.

Theodore frowned. "Why would I tell you anything? I don't even know your name."

She straightened in her chair. "I'm Cynthia. I travel with Juliet Jasper. She's a VIP guest here at the hotel—a very important person. She won an Oscar for a movie, you know," she added in a condescending manner.

"Yeah? How long ago was that?" The minute the words left Theodore's mouth, he wished he could take them back. *No matter how rude our esteemed guests behave, the doorman never expresses his disapproval."* Theodore glanced guiltily around the room, but Grandfather was nowhere to be seen. He rose from his chair. "I'm sorry. I have to get back to my post."

Cynthia gave him a crafty smile. "That's right, you're just the doorman."

Theodore kept his mouth closed, but angry words gathered in his head. This particular guest was impossible—especially when he wanted to be so much more than a doorman to Lila.

CHAPTER FOUR

The afternoon sped by as Theodore greeted guests and bid others goodbye. It wasn't until he was relieved at suppertime that he finally had a moment to address the thought that had been bothering him all day. Had someone tried to harm, or even kill Zanna, as Lila suspected? The idea of a killer in the hotel was serious business. They might all be in danger.

Theodore decided to investigate on his own. He knew Grandfather would not approve of his taking time away from his duties to find the answer, so he'd do his investigation during the evening hours when he was off.

That evening, he ate in the cafeteria with his family as he normally would, but then he got up to leave.

"Hey! Where are you going?" asked one of his brothers. "Won't you play ball with me?"

Theodore shook his head. "Not tonight, little bro." He waved goodbye to his family and headed out of the room. Bandit was arriving as Theodore made his exit.

"Yo! How's it goin'?" Bandit didn't bother to wait for an answer, but headed right over to Lila's table.

Theodore watched him, wondering what it was about Bandit that made him so appealing to Lila. Sure, he had muscles and was considered very cool, but he didn't seem Lila's type.

His mother approached him. "Remember, Theodore," she warned him softly, "no socializing with the hotel guests."

Theodore nodded sadly and went to his room, where he changed into jeans and a black turtleneck. Determination filled him. He wasn't sure how to go about finding clues, but he had to do something to win Lila's heart and to keep everyone safe.

He decided to start in Zanna's room. He scurried up, up, up through the plumbing of the hotel, to the very spot where he and Lila had entered her room. He crawled through the hole and pushed so hard against the loose piece of baseboard inside the closet that he toppled onto the carpet. He was about to head for the half-open door when he noticed a mouse-like shadow behind one of Zanna's silvery shoes.

He crept over to it and pounced. "Gotcha!"

"Squeeak!" Cynthia glared at him and adjusted her glasses. "What did you do that for? And just what, may I ask, are you doing here, Doorman?"

"That's for me to know, not you," Theodore said snappishly. Cynthia brought out the worst in him, but she was so irritating he couldn't help himself. Theodore heard Zanna's sweet voice in the background and the deeper tones of a man. Suspicion growing, he turned to Cynthia. "Why are you listening to them?" Was she the one who'd put alcohol in Zanna's glass?

Cynthia gave him a smug look. "I not only can read human language, I can write it. Juliet isn't always aware of it, but I help her find stuff out and leave her notes. It's important to our career. Uh, I mean *her* career."

"Ah, so you're her little spy. That's not very nice." He himself knew how to read the people's words, but he'd refused to learn how to write it. Now, he wished he'd listened to his teacher.

Cynthia clamped her paws on her hips and glared at him. "Not nice you say? So why are you here? Huh?"

Theodore tried to think of a quick reply, but couldn't think of any. He certainly didn't want Cynthia to know he was investigating a possible attempt at murder. Not when she could be the very one who did it.

"Just stay out of my way," Cynthia warned.

Theodore sighed and did his best to ignore her. He couldn't leave. He had to find out who Zanna was talking to. He crept to the door and peeked around its frame.

Samuel Horner, the producer, was sitting in a chair by the window. Zanna sat on the couch, facing him.

"You gave us a real scare," the producer said to Zanna. "I thought you might have to go home. Simone has been after me to give her the starring role in the movie, but I'm not so sure she's the one I want for it."

Zanna pressed her lips together. "That woman would do anything to get that part. And Juliet is no better." She lifted an ice pack to her bruised eye.

Theodore noticed Cynthia taking notes. The film business was not as much fun as some people made it seem. Everyone, it appeared, wanted the same thing and would do anything to get their way.

Sam rose. "Well, we've got all week to iron things out. It's important for all of us to get along, even if we have to pretend to be friends. We need to do whatever it takes to make this movie; it's one of the best scripts I've read in a long, long time."

They were staying in the hotel for a week? Theodore's spirits lifted. That would give him a whole week to win Lila's heart.

Zanna drew up from the couch, capturing Theodore's attention. "I'll be all right, Sam. Don't worry. I'm not giving up on working hard for that wonderful role in your movie."

Cynthia put away her pen and paper. "See you later, Doorman. Don't linger too long. Lila is downstairs with her boyfriend, but they might arrive at any moment."

She made her way through the hole in the wall, leaving Theodore alone. He sank down on the carpet and clasped his face with his paw, deep in thought. It appeared not one person, but two would be glad if Zanna didn't get the part in the movie. But did that mean Simone or Juliet had tried to kill her?

CHAPTER FIVE

Theodore was about to leave the closet when a knock came at the door to Zanna's room. He paused as Zanna went to open it.

A maid stood there. "Turn-down service, Ma'am."

While the maid gathered fresh towels from her cart and headed for the bathroom, Zanna went back to the couch and flipped through a magazine. Theodore was about to leave when a movement on the maid's cart caught his eye. A familiar white head appeared behind a roll of fluffy, white toilet paper. His heart pounded with alarm. Lila!

She looked over at him and frowned. Quick as can be, she jumped down from the cart, scurried across the carpet, and into the closet.

"What are you doing here?" she asked in a tone that didn't sound too friendly.

He swallowed nervously. "I'm trying to find out if anyone actually tried to harm Zanna."

Lila's demeanor instantly changed. Her eyes moistened as she clasped her paws together. "You would do that for her?"

"I ... I ..." he stuttered, wishing Lila would understand he was doing it for *her*, not Zanna.

"That's so very thoughtful! How wonderful! I'll even help you." Lila flashed him a smile. "You don't mind, do you?"

Theodore shook his head, too shy to say anything.

"So, how do we start?" Lila said.

"We need to investigate all the stars and the producer. Someone doesn't want Zanna to get the starring role in the movie. It could be any one of them."

Lila frowned. "Yes, it sometimes is a nasty business. When do we begin?"

Theodore checked his watch. "I've got to get back to my family. We'll start tomorrow night. I'll meet you here after dinner."

"Thanks." Lila gave him a deliciously wide smile that warmed his racing heart.

As he found his way back to the nest his mother had made for the family, Theodore couldn't help humming a song. Just when he thought things were going to get worse, they got better. Lila and he were a team now.

The next evening, Theodore choked down his dinner, barely able to recall the day's comings and goings from the doorman's post. He'd checked his watch all afternoon, wondering when his shift would be over. Each minute had seemed like an hour.

Lila wasn't in the dining room. He suspected she might be as excited as he to take on the job of detective.

He got up from the table and waved goodbye to his mother. "I've got to go. See you later."

His mother gave him a questioning look, but, to his relief, she made no comment nor asked any questions.

As he walked away from the table, he noticed Cynthia staring at him. Careful not to appear too anxious to leave the room, he strolled toward the entrance and ... bumped into Maurice.

"Sorry," Theodore said.

Maurice glanced at him, but made no comment. Instead, he hurried to get into the food line. Theodore shook his head. Maurice was one weird mouse. So far, he'd never heard a squeak out of him.

Making sure no one was tailing him, Theodore entered the plumbing system and raced up the pipes to Zanna's room. He took a moment outside to brush off his uniform and smooth back the fur on his face, and then he entered the closet. He looked around expecting to see Lila, but she was nowhere to be found. Puzzled, Theodore studied the area once more.

A shadow emerged from the corner of the closet.

Theodore jumped with surprise.

A soft, tinkling laugh filled the air. "Oh, good! Did I scare you?"

Lila tiptoed toward him. A black kerchief was tied around her head. She was dressed in a black sweater and black pants. "How do I look?" She twirled around. "Detectives like us can't be seen. Right?"

"Right," said Theodore, thinking she looked adorable.

"I've been thinking about this," said Lila. "We need to begin our investigation with Simone. I'm sure she's the one who gave Zanna some kind of drug. I want to prove it and report it to the producer."

"Okay, we'll start there," said Theodore, "but real detectives don't make up their minds about a case until they have all the evidence."

"Oh, right, but I'm sure it's Simone." Lila gave him a big smile. "Call it women's intuition."

Theodore shook his head. Working with Lila wasn't going to be as easy as he'd thought. "Do you know the way to her room?"

She nodded. "Follow me. It's just down the hall from Zanna. #2410."

Theodore peeked out through the opening in the closet door. "Where's Zanna now?"

"She's gone out to dinner with the others. Simone, Juliet,

and Rocky came to her room to talk, and then they decided to try a new restaurant."

"I see. Simone's room could be free now, but what about Fifi? If that nasty dog is inside Simone's room, we'll have to search a different place."

Lila waved away his concern. "We'll be fine. Fifi goes everywhere with her."

They scurried across the living room. Stepping into the hallway, Theodore almost stumbled onto a tray sitting on the floor outside the door.

"They had room service?" Theodore asked.

Lila nodded.

Theodore studied the tray. An empty wine bottle, three used wine glasses, and a cup and saucer sat atop it. Lila had told him Zanna didn't drink, so if the other three had wine, the coffee cup must have been used by Zanna, proving she doesn't drink alcohol. He'd smelled alcohol along with something else in the glass beside Zanna's bed. Another reason to suspect she might have been drugged.

"Hurry!" whispered Lila. "A maid is coming down the hall."

Staying as close as possible to the walls, the two mice ran down the carpeted hallway.

A sliver of light shone into the hallway from the bottom of the door at room 2410. Theodore studied the space. It looked too narrow for them to slide through.

The rattle of the maid's cart sounded closer and closer.

Theodore's heart pounded. If either he or Lila were discovered, the whole mouse colony would be in trouble.

"I think I can make it." Lila lay on her belly and inched her way through.

Theodore sucked in his stomach, pushed into the opening, and came to a stop. One arm and one leg stuck out through the opening. "Help me, Lila!" he squeaked.

Lila grabbed hold of him.

"Hurry!"

Pulling and scrambling together, Theodore made it under the door and into the room just as the maid's cart came to a noisy stop nearby. Letting out a sigh of relief, he stood and straightened his uniform. His gaze swept the room. It was dimly lit by a tableside lamp next to an overstuffed chair. All was quiet.

"What do we do now?" Lila asked, clasping her paws together eagerly.

"Check the area for any sign of drugs. We have to be quick. The maid is next door."

They sprinted for the bathroom.

"Detective work is so exciting!" Lila gushed, stopping to straighten her sweater.

"Better keep up with me," Theodore warned her. "We have to get in and get out of here before anyone comes."

"Oh, right." Lila gave him a wide grin and followed him up onto the vanity counter.

A large number of bottles and jars were scattered atop the surface. Theodore studied the pots of blush and wands of mascara. He looked over the skin creams and bottles of makeup. But he saw no sign of anything that could be used to drug Zanna.

"I wonder what Simone really looks like underneath all that makeup. My Zanna doesn't need all this stuff. She's beautiful as she is." An unmistakable note of pride filled Lila's voice.

Theodore checked his watch. "C'mon! Let's go! The maid will be here any minute, and we have to check out the other rooms."

A knock at the door froze them in place.

"What are we going to do?" whispered Lila. "We're as far away from the door as possible."

Theodore held a paw to his lips.

The door opened. "Maid service. Anyone here?"

At the silence, the maid walked inside, carrying clean towels.

"Hide!" said Theodore. "She's coming in here." He jumped down to the floor and tucked himself in the shadows behind the toilet. He turned, expecting to see Lila behind him.

"Lila? Where are you?" he squeaked softly.

He saw movement in the bunch of used towels thrown into the corner of the room. He was about to call out a warning when the soft-soled black shoes of the maid appeared next to him. Too late!

The maid grabbed the used towels and threw them, along with Lila, onto the cart ...

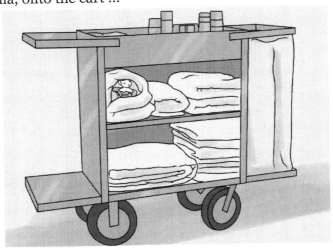

... and then into a clear plastic bag. Theodore's heart skipped a beat. He waited for a sign of movement inside the bag, but all was still. His pulse pounded with dismay. Had

Lila been injured by the weight of the wet towels on top of her? Or worse, smashed to death?

The flushing of the toilet sent Theodore cowering behind it. Worried sick about Lila, he huddled there as the maid continued to give the bathroom a quick freshening.

Moments later, the maid picked up the bag and left the room. The slamming of the door sent Theodore racing to it. Panic helped him squeeze under the door and into the hallway. He had to save Lila.

CHAPTER SIX

The maid stood by her cart talking to another woman—someone she called Mary.

"Better let me take those wet towels to the laundry," Mary said. "I've got a bunch of my own to take down to the basement."

No-o-o-o! Theodore screamed in his mind. Trapped like that, how would Lila ever escape?

The maid handed Mary her bag of towels. Horrified, Theodore watched Mary toss Lila and the bag of towels onto her cart and wheel it away.

As soon as the maid left the hallway, Theodore raced as fast as he could after the cart. At the sound of people approaching, he stretched out alongside the gray-painted baseboard. He lay there trembling, hoping his dark uniform would help hide him.

Footsteps came closer and closer.

Theodore's heart pounded with alarm. He had to save Lila! Where was she now? How would he ever find her?

"Hey, look!" said a young girl, pointing at him. "That looks like a mouse! A mouse wearing a funny costume!"

Theodore's whole body weakened inside his stiff uniform. He couldn't decide whether to run or stay still.

"Don't be silly," said her mother, tugging on the girl's arm. "You're just making up more stories. Come along now. We can't dawdle. You've caused enough problems as it is." Her mother marched her along the hallway. The girl looked back at Theodore and waved.

As soon as the hall was clear once more, Theodore took

off following the route the cart had taken down the long hallway and around the corner. He came to a stop in front of a sign that said *Service Elevator*. His heart fell. He couldn't manage to ride on an elevator without help.

The sound of a cart rolling toward him sent him into the shadows of the nearby corner. Hope filled him when he noticed two bags of soiled towels mounded on top of the cart. As soon as it rolled to a stop, Theodore took a deep breath and scurried aboard. He poked his way between a box of soaps and a box of silver-wrapped chocolates and hunkered down. Normally, the smell of chocolate would excite him. Not tonight. His stomach was tied in worried knots.

The elevator doors opened.

As the maid pushed the cart inside, Theodore clung to the boxes, telling himself not to be scared. But when doors closed behind them, and the elevator began its descent, Theodore held back a squeak of dismay. He knew about elevators, of course, but he'd never ridden in one. The ride made his stomach feel squishy inside, as if he'd eaten a big piece of spongy marshmallow.

The elevator stopped and the doors opened. The maid pushed the cart out into a room alive with sound and heat. From his place on the cart, Theodore gazed at the many mounds of white sheets and towels scattered about the floor. His throat closed with worry. How, he wondered, would he ever find Lila in all this confusion?

He jumped off the cart and raced over to a bunch of towels piled in front of one of several large, stainless-steel, washing machines. Through the front glass window of the machine, he saw towels swished around and around in soapy, deadly circles. The thought of Lila ending her life in such a way made Theodore's knees wobbly. He sank onto the floor and held his head in his paws. It was *his* fault. He never should have accepted Lila's offer to help him. He'd done it because he'd wanted to spend time with her and have a chance to win her heart. She was the most beautiful mouse he'd ever seen, and now, she might be dead!

He forced himself to his feet and rushed from one pile of towels to another, trying to stay out of view as he continued his hopeless search. Sadness filled him. What would he say to the others when they found out what had happened? He sank to the floor once more, not caring how dangerously dark his uniform was against the white of the towels.

A light tap on his shoulder brought him to his feet. He whipped around.

"What are you doing down here? It's dangerous with all these people," squeaked a familiar voice.

Theodore didn't stop to think about it. He pulled Lila into his arms and kissed her. When he realized what he'd done, he pushed her away. "I'm sorry ... Miss ... Lila ... I thought I'd lost you!"

Lila's pink eyes were round with surprise. "No, no. I understand. It's been a difficult night. We'll just pretend this didn't happen."

Theodore nodded, but he would never forget how right she felt in his embrace. But he knew nothing would come of it. It couldn't. She was a hotel guest, and he was not.

He focused once more on their situation. "C'mon! We've got to get out of here." He grabbed hold of Lila's paw and tugged her toward the door.

"Where are we going?"

"I think I know a way into the alley."

Lila pulled him to a stop and gave him a worried look. "But ... but ... isn't that where your father was killed?"

He gulped and nodded. "Yes, but what choice do we have? If we go up the stairs, we'll be on the main floor of the hotel.

And if any people see us, all of us mice will be kicked out of here before we can even pack."

Lila gave him a grim look. "You're right. We can't ruin The Winston for everyone else because we got ourselves trapped down here."

They scurried along the tile hallway to the door leading outside. Smokers used the alley behind the hotel as a gathering place. If they were lucky, the door would be cracked open.

No such luck.

Theodore and Lila waited in the shadows, breathing hard from their race for freedom.

After several minutes of hiding, the door to the alley opened. Black sneakers, worn below black-checkered pants, entered the building. A hotel cook walked right by them.

Theodore grabbed Lila's paw, and they hurried into the alley.

Pausing in the dark, smelly alley, Theodore's body turned cold with fear. He'd been warned time and time again to stay away from there.

"We have to find our way to the front of the building," he said. "That's the safest place for us to enter the hotel."

"But it's scary out here." Lila gripped his paw tighter.

At the panic in her pink eyes, Theodore swallowed hard. "Come on, let's go. And, Lila, no matter what happens, don't stop running!"

Paw in paw, they took off.

"I don't like this," puffed Lila, working hard to keep pace with him.

They were running free and clear, sticking as close as they could to the building when a large, black tom cat bounded toward them.

"EEEEKKK!" Lila dropped Theodore's paw and scurried

behind a garbage bin, squeaking all the way.

Theodore followed her. He tried to climb the metal container, but it was too slippery and he fell back down with a squeak of dismay.

"Under here," said Lila. The metal feet of the garbage bin held it off the floor a mere two inches. She ran into the space.

Theodore crawled in beside her and sat, trying to catch his breath.

"Look out!" squeaked Lila.

The cat's black paw stretched under the bin and swiped at the ground where they were sitting, knocking Theodore onto his back. The cat's other paw reached for Lila. A long, sharp claw caught on the fabric of her pants.

"Meow!" cried the cat, triumphantly, dragging her to him.

"Help!" cried Lila, struggling to find a foothold on the pavement.

Theodore rolled to his feet and grabbed hold of Lila. A tug of war began between him and the cat. Lila's pants ripped, releasing her from the claw that held them. Theodore tugged as hard as he could, and Lila fell back, free.

"You did it!" cried Lila, scurrying out of range of the cat's paw.

But the cat wasn't about to give up. Several times, it tried to reach into the space to grab them.

Miserable, Theodore and Lila huddled together.

At the sound of another cat's meows, the claws of the black tomcat disappeared. The cats began hissing at one another. Soon, deafening yowls filled the air.

"They're fighting. Let's make a break for it!" Theodore crawled to the edge of the bin and peeked out. A large, yellow tiger cat and the black one were clawing at each other.

Theodore waved Lila forward. "Follow me!"

Side by side, they darted down the alley. At each step, Theodore felt as if a claw was about to nab him from behind. He couldn't help glancing over his shoulder. Beside him, Lila looked as terrified as he felt.

They'd just rounded the corner to the front of the hotel when they heard a noise behind them. Not one cat, but two bore down on them. Theodore led the way down the well-worn path behind the bushes lining the front of the hotel. At a steady run, they swung through the mouse's revolving entrance, twirling around and around until they landed on the floor inside.

"Hey, you cats! Get out of here!" roared the people's doorman. He chased them away.

A sigh of relief rumbled up from the depths of Theodore's body. He turned to Lila. "Are you all right?"

"Yes, but I've never been so scared in my life."

"Me, either," Theodore admitted.

"You were trying awfully hard to be brave," said Lila. "Thanks."

It was almost a compliment, thought Theodore, wishing for more. He walked Lila to the plumbing area and waited until she was safely on her way to Zanna's room before heading home to his family.

Later, lying in his bed, Theodore thought of all that had happened. He and Lila had almost lost their lives. If that had happened, his family would be left with no means to survive. He couldn't do that to them. He'd promised his mother that he'd always be there for her and his siblings. As sorry as he was about Zanna's situation, he decided his detective days had to end.

CHAPTER SEVEN

"Theodore! Wake up!"

Theodore blinked sleepily at his mother and squinted at the bedside clock. His eyes widened. He'd have just enough time to get dressed and run to his post. Another day without breakfast.

He jumped out of bed. It had been an awful night. His nightmares had been full of cats chasing him and catching him in their claws. It brought back sad memories. One dark and stormy night, his gentle, loving father had lost a fight with such a cat.

His mother frowned at him. "Are you all right, Theodore?"

He nodded. "Just late." He couldn't tell her what he'd been doing.

Grandfather was already at the doorman's post when Theodore arrived there out of breath. Grandfather pointed to his watch and smiled. "Just in time, Theodore. I'm glad. Beau Beady is after your job, so it's important you're prompt. You can take over now."

Theodore frowned. Beau Beady was a year younger and constantly trying to outdo him. In fact, those beady eyes of Beau's seemed to catch every little mistake Theodore made.

It being a Saturday morning and an early hour, traffic was slow. Then a group of men and women carrying cameras and microphones gathered in front of the hotel.

Grandfather approached Theodore. "Be on your toes. Reporters are here, trying to get an interview with Zanna. Word is out that she tried to kill herself."

Theodore frowned. He was pretty sure Zanna hadn't tried to kill herself. Someone else had wanted to harm her. Lila knew Zanna best, and she was convinced of it. So was he.

Noise and the light from flashbulbs erupted as Zanna emerged from the hotel. Theodore studied her. Accompanied by Samuel Horner, she was still pale, but looked as beautiful as ever. She wore a simple black dress and carried a large, tan purse.

The questions came at Zanna one atop another.

"Zanna, is it true? Did you try to kill yourself?" cried one reporter.

"Is it because you and Rocky Strong are fighting?" asked another.

"Is your relationship with Rocky over?" said still another.

"I heard Simone Skinner is going to take the starring role from you in Sam's upcoming movie. If not her, Juliet Jasper. Is that true?"

Sam held up his hand. "Ladies and gentlemen of the press, Zanna is fine. You can see that for yourself. Now please allow us to get into the limo. This sweet lady deserves a chance to do some shopping."

The hotel's general manager came outside to speak to the reporters. "Step aside. Please do not interfere with our guests. They are due respect and privacy, which we at The Winston Hotel honor. I ask you to do the same."

Amid the reporters' grumbling, Zanna and Sam Horner slipped into the white limousine that had quietly rolled up to the front entrance.

Theodore watched the limo take off and turned to Grandfather. "I don't think Zanna tried to kill herself like they say. I think someone tried to hurt her."

Grandfather gave him a steady look. "That's for others to work out. Not us."

Theodore nodded. After his horrifying experiences with Lila last night and with Grandfather's warning ringing in his head, he decided to let others do detective work.

At break time, Theodore hurried into the cafeteria. It had been a long time between meals, and his stomach was pinched with hunger. He stood in line looking over the selection of food scraps when he felt a tap on his shoulder. He turned, expecting to see Lila. At the appearance of Juliet's assistant, Theodore hid a disappointed groan.

Cynthia stood next to him, her eyes rounder than usual behind her glasses. "Theodore, can I speak to you? Alone?"

He couldn't stop feeling cross. "What do you want, Cynthia? I have just a few minutes before I have to get back to my post. I'm the doorman. Remember?"

She nodded. "I know. I'm sorry I was mean to you, but, really, I need your help."

Theodore loaded his tray and carried it over to a table for two. Cynthia followed at his heels. "Please, Theodore."

He let out a sigh. "You might as well sit down and talk to me while I eat."

Cynthia took a seat opposite him and glanced around the room. "I don't want anyone else to hear this. Juliet is very sick. I think someone poisoned her. Lila caught me crying, and when I told her what had happened, she said to come to you. She said you're doing some detective work together. Is it true?"

"Not anymore. We almost got killed last night."

"But she said you promised to help her. I want you to help me too. Without Juliet, I have nothing to live for. Working for her is my entire life." Tears rolled down Cynthia's dull gray cheeks.

Sympathy defiantly welled up in Theodore. If Juliet was poisoned, someone in the hotel must have been responsible. It was a mystery he couldn't ignore. But was it worth getting killed over? He had his family to take care of. What would they do without him? But then again, if they had a serial killer on their hands, the hotel and everyone in it might be in trouble.

Cynthia got to her feet. "Just think about it. Lila has all the details. She said she'd talk it over with you when you got off work."

Shoulders slumped, Cynthia walked away oblivious of the curious stares of others.

Though his stomach had begun to churn with anxiety, Theodore forced food down. How could he disappoint Cynthia? How could he tell Lila his detective days were over? They both believed in him.

Zanna and Sam returned to the hotel sometime later, each carrying a number of shopping bags. Seeing Zanna laugh and smile, Theodore wondered what would have happened if he and Lila hadn't come to her rescue. A shiver snaked up and down his furry back.

He noticed a movement from one of the many pockets in the enormous tan leather purse slung over Zanna's shoulder. Lila lifted her head out of the pocket, glanced around and waved at him.

He could feel his lips spread into a wide grin. She was as spunky as she was beautiful. Whenever he saw her, his heart sped up in a burst of happiness. Feeling all fuzzy and warm inside, he vowed to do anything she asked.

Zanna stood in front of the hotel talking to one of her fans. The reporters rushed toward the scene. The clicking of their cameras and the flashing of lights made Theodore wince.

Amid all the noise and confusion, Lila squeaked, "I need to talk to you."

Theodore nodded. There was no way he'd let her down. Scared or not, he was about to embark on another detective mission.

As soon as his shift at the door ended, Theodore hurried into the cafeteria. He and Lila had to come up with a plan. But first, he needed to fill his belly for energy. As he was loading his tray with a mound of food, he noticed Lila sitting with Cynthia at a corner table. He turned away from their stares. He couldn't let anyone on the hotel staff find out he was interacting with guests.

He took a seat at the table with his family.

"Hi, Theodore!" said one of his little sisters. The smile she gave him tugged at his heart strings. He could not jeopardize his job. She and all the other mousekins needed him.

"My, you're hungry tonight," said his mother. Her eyes shone with approval. "You're growing so well, Theodore. The boys are hoping you'll have time for a ball game."

Theodore shook his head. "Not tonight."

His mother frowned. "Is everything all right? You didn't get in until late last night. That's not like you."

"I just need some time to myself," he said, fully aware she'd disapprove of his detective work.

The frown on his mother's face was replaced by a look of embarrassment. "Oh, yes, of course. After all you do for us, it's important for you to have some fun. Just be careful."

Theodore let out a sigh of relief. He'd hate to disappoint her or anyone else in his family. Out of the corner of his eye, he noticed Lila and Cynthia leaving the cafeteria.

"See you later," he said to his family, and rose to his feet.

As Theodore was leaving, Maurice entered the cafeteria, glanced at him, and shuffled over to the cafeteria line. Theodore drew his eyebrows together thoughtfully. Most of the guests acknowledged him with a wave or a squeak. Not Maurice.

When Theodore stepped out into the hallway, Cynthia and Lila signaled for him to follow them.

"Come quickly," said Cynthia. "I've reserved the small conference room. We can talk in there."

The three of them sprinted down the hall and into a small paneled room. Cynthia locked the door and turned to them with a sigh. "Lila, like I told you this morning, I found Juliet very sick. I've never seen her so bad." Her lip quivered. "I thought she was going to die."

Theodore gave her a skeptical look. "What did she do last night? Have too much to eat or drink?"

Cynthia shook her head. "That's just it. She decided not to go out to dinner with everyone else. She had room service bring her up a light dinner, took a headache pill like she always does, and went to bed. A little bit later, she began to throw up. It lasted all night."

"Maybe she was just coming down with the flu," Theodore said. "Sounds like it to me."

"Just wait," said Lila, placing a paw on his arm. "She has more to tell us."

Cynthia took a deep breath. "There was something so wrong about it that I became concerned. That's when I bumped into Lila."

Lila nodded.

"This afternoon, Juliet seemed much better. I heard her tell someone on the phone that she was going to take another headache pill and would try to catch up on her sleep."

"So?" said Theodore. This didn't sound like a cause for alarm.

Lila frowned at him. "There's more. Go ahead and tell him, Cynthia."

"I checked on her just before dinner and she was really, really sick again." Cynthia squeezed her eyes. Two tears rolled down her cheeks. "Juliet never gets sick. Something's wrong. I know it."

Lila gave him a bright smile. "I told her we'd help figure it out."

In response to Lila's hopeful look, Theodore couldn't help the way his lips curved. But his heart sank. Things did not sound good at all. Someone was making trouble. Big trouble.

CHAPTER EIGHT

The three mice detectives left the conference room and hurried along the hallway, hoping no one would spy them. It might start rumors of all kinds, and good detectives did not bring attention to themselves.

They entered the plumbing system. Theodore let Cynthia take the lead. She wove them through a maze of pipes, ending in a wing of the hotel building Theodore had never seen.

"This is Juliet's room, right behind here," Cynthia announced.

Lila frowned. "But isn't this Mr. Horner's room?"

Cynthia shook her head. "Mr. Horner is in room 2498A. This is 2498B. They're both part of the Presidential suite." A look of pride crossed her face. "Juliet deserves the best."

"And usually gets it," said Lila with a touch of disgust.

"She's the one who got an Oscar. Not Zanna," retorted Cynthia.

Theodore placed a paw on each of their shoulders. "This isn't the time to bicker. We've got more important things to take care of. Remember?"

Lila and Cynthia gave him sheepish expressions and nodded.

"Follow me," said Cynthia. "There's a space beneath the baseboard in one of the bathrooms." She poked her head through a narrow opening in the wall and turned back to them. "The coast is clear."

Lila followed Cynthia into the hole and disappeared. Sucking in his stomach, Theodore forced his body through the small space and entered a dimly lit bathroom.

"Where does Juliet keep her sleeping pills?" Theodore asked Cynthia. He glanced around, but couldn't see any sign of pills there.

"She keeps them by her bed? Why?"

"I'm thinking the person who gave Zanna bad medicine is doing the same thing to Juliet. They're sick in a different way, of course, but it's the same method."

Cynthia's eyes widened behind her glasses. "Of course! That must be it!"

"He's the best detective I know," said Lila, giving him a wide smile.

At the compliment, Theodore's cheeks felt warm. "You two stay here. I'll go check on her." He couldn't help the swagger that entered his step as he made his way to the door of the bathroom and looked out.

He blinked in surprise. This was no ordinary hotel room. Couches and plush chairs sat atop a colorful rug. A grand piano stood in the corner of the room, a fancy desk in another. Bowls of fresh flowers were everywhere.

"This looks like a living room. Where's the bedroom? Where's Juliet?"

Cynthia gave him a smug smile. "I told you this was part of the Presidential Suite. It's very special—fit for a president. It has four bathrooms, two living rooms and three bedrooms. Hers is down the hall. Follow me."

Lila and Theodore scampered silently behind Cynthia, who led them into a bedroom much larger than Zanna's. Standing in the shadows at the doorway, Theodore quickly sized up the situation. Fully dressed, Juliet lay sprawled atop the sheets on a king-size bed. She was groaning softly. A bedside table sat on either side of the bed. He paused. They'd have to split up to find the pills.

"You two take the table on the left. I'll take the one on the right. We need to get hold of the headache pills. I suspect those pills might be making her ill."

Keeping an eye on Juliet, Theodore made his way to the table on the right. He paused to study her. The skin on her face had a greenish tone to it. Was it food poisoning? Or did it have something to do with the pills like he'd first suspected? Either way, from the look of her, she had to feel miserable.

Juliet suddenly sat up in bed, her blue eyes as big as the Frisbees young guests sometimes carried into the hotel. A terrible rumbling noise came from her middle. She gazed around the room wildly.

In terror, he stood frozen.

"Oh, no! I'm going to be sick again," whimpered Juliet. She covered her mouth with her hand. One foot, then another hit the floor near Theodore with such force he felt the air stir around him. He barely had time to jump out of the way of her feet as she dashed out of the room.

With Juliet out of the room, Theodore scampered up onto the bed and onto the bedside table. He searched for the pills, but he found nothing but a box of tissues. He looked across the bed at Lila and Cynthia. They'd managed to open the drawer to the bedside table and were peering inside it.

"It's here!" said Lila.

"In the drawer," added Cynthia.

Juliet raced back into the room, threw herself down on the bed, lifted her head groggily and reached for the glass of water on the table beside Lila and Cynthia.

With barely concealed squeaks, Lila and Cynthia dove into the drawer.

Theodore watched helplessly as Juliet mumbled something, slammed the drawer shut, and replaced the glass on the table. Laying her head back on her pillow, she closed her eyes. After several tense moments of waiting, Theodore heard snores coming from Juliet's mouth.

Balancing carefully on the narrow wooden headboard, Theodore cautiously began to make his way across the top of the bed's headboard. Trying to keep his balance, he teetered back and forth, like a tight- wire walker in a circus act. He stopped and took a deep breath. One slip and he'd land on Juliet's head.

"Theodore! Help us!" Lila squeaked, pounding on the front of the drawer.

"Shhh! I'm coming," he said, barely catching himself from falling.

"Hurry!" called Cynthia. "I don't like being trapped in here." Her voice was muffled, but it was clear she was panicking.

He'd just made it to the far side of the bed when Juliet cried out in her sleep and swung a hand out, shaking the headboard. Theodore clung to the bedpost, hiding as best he could behind it as Juliet's eyes flipped open. She stared glassily around the room and closed her eyes again.

Theodore waited a few moments for her to settle down, and then he scurried onto the table top, coming to a skidding stop atop the smooth surface.

"Open up," said Cynthia. "I feel as if I can't breathe."

"Hurry, Theodore," Lila implored him.

Theodore stretched out atop the table, leaned over the edge, and tugged on the knob of the drawer as hard as he could. It barely moved.

"You're going to have to help!" he whispered. "At the count of three, push as hard as you can, using all your weight against the drawer. I'll pull. Ready? One ... two ... three!"

The drawer flew open so fast, it almost threw the two mice inside it onto the floor.

"Hang on!" cried Theodore. "Now give me that bottle. We've got to move fast!"

A knock sounded at the door. "Juliet? Are you all right?" called a familiar voice.

Cynthia pushed the bottle of pills onto the floor and raced down the leg of the night table. Lila followed her.

The door opened a crack.

Theodore jumped from the table to the floor, bracing himself for a hard fall. Thick carpeting helped to soften his landing, but the breath was knocked out of him. He lay on the dark carpet, gasping for air.

Cynthia and Lila rolled the bottle of pills under the bed.

Still fighting for breath, Theodore quickly followed them into the shadows.

Footsteps came closer to the bed. "Juliet? It's Sam. What's happened to you? Did you eat something bad?"

The mattress creaked. Juliet's feet appeared at the side of the bed. "I'm not sure what it is, but I've never been sicker."

"What will I tell the people at the television studio? You were supposed to do an interview this evening."

"I don't care what you tell them, I can't do it. Understand?" she snarled angrily.

Sam let out a long sigh. "This week was supposed to produce a lot of support for the new movie—financial support I need. Instead, it's been one problem after another."

The actress moaned. "Just leave. I think I'm going to be sick again." In a split second, Juliet was on her feet and sprinting for the bathroom.

"Ugh, you really are sick. I'll send up someone to help you." Sam left the room, slamming the door behind him.

Beneath the bed, the mice went into action, tugging on

the cap of the pill bottle. "Hurry! Let's see what's inside, and then we have to get out of here," said Theodore.

White capsules spilled onto the carpet beside the bed.

"They all look the same," said Cynthia. "You were wrong, Theodore. There's no problem with them."

"Don't be too sure." Theodore held up a capsule. A tiny X was marked on it. Looking through the stash of pills, he found a few others marked the same way. "I bet these have something inside that shouldn't be there."

He pulled open the capsule. Orange powder fell out.

Lila handed him one without an X on it. The powder that tumbled out of it was a pale purple.

Theodore nodded. "Just as I thought. Someone has tampered with Juliet's medicine. I bet they put the bad ones right on top."

Lila shook his arm for attention. "Uh, oh. Juliet's coming back."

They waited until Juliet was lying down again before they scampered to the door and out of the room. In the small, private bathroom where they'd entered the suite, they huddled together.

"Something serious is going on, and I think I know who might be at the bottom of this," Cynthia said.

Lila clasped her paws together. "Who?"

Cynthia's features formed an angry scowl. "Who do you think? Simone!"

Theodore stroked his chin thoughtfully. "It makes sense. With the other two stars out of the way, she'd get the starring role in the movie."

"What can we do about it?" asked Lila.

"I know exactly what to do," said Cynthia. "We'll write her a note warning her to cease and desist, as lawyers might say."

Lila and Theodore looked at each other.

"You can write?" said Theodore, impressed in spite of himself.

"Of course I can," scoffed Cynthia. "Can't you?"

Theodore ignored the mocking look on Cynthia's face. "It's a good plan. Once she knows we're onto her, she'll have to stop."

They hurried back to the living room in the suite and went right over to the desk.

"Help me drag a piece of stationery downstairs. I'll work on the note tonight," Cynthia commanded.

"Okay," said Lila, "but don't give it to her before Theodore and I have a chance to see it."

Cynthia rolled her eyes.

"We're in this together. Remember?" said Theodore, trying to hide his irritation. It was sometimes hard to like Cynthia very much.

Between the three of them, they were able to drag the sheet of paper to the bathroom, where they folded it neatly so it could go through the small hole in the wall.

They jiggled and juggled the piece of paper through the system of pipes. By the time they entered the mouse hotel, Theodore wasn't at all sure how they'd get it back up to Simone's room.

Leaving Lila and Cynthia in the small conference room, he rushed to his home. His brothers and sisters would be waiting for him. Thursday night was storytelling time.

As soon as he entered the extended nest he called home, his mother gave him an inquiring glance. He nodded to her, but said nothing. He was breaking the rules, but it was for a good cause. If he told her that attempted murders were taking place in the hotel, she'd want to take his siblings and leave. Then what would happen to them? He couldn't take a chance on his family being destitute, or out in the cold, or, heaven forbid, caught in the alley.

"Hi, Theodore!" said one of his brothers. "Are you ready to read us a story? How about The Littlest Mousekin?"

Theodore grinned. This particular brother never got tired of the story about a tiny mouse that saves his family from a gigantic tomcat.

Long after the little ones were sound asleep and his mother and grandfather had retired for the night, Theodore lay awake. Simone wasn't a pleasant person, but was she a murderer?

CHAPTER NINE

At his post the next morning, Theodore stifled a yawn. A pair of familiar, highly polished shoes appeared outside the entry. The general manager greeted the doorman for the humans without his usual jovial voice. "How are things going here, Pete?"

"We're not as busy as we usually are," Pete replied. "I don't know what the problem is. What do you think?"

The GM hesitated then said, "Well, the publicity over Zanna Loverly's illness couldn't have helped us. And now Juliet Jasper is claiming she got food poisoning here."

"Movie stars! Who needs them," snorted the doorman.

The GM shook a finger at him. "We don't want any of our guests to have a bad experience here. Remember that. The ownership isn't above selling this hotel if they don't get the financial returns they want every month."

Pete straightened. "Yes, Sir, I'll remember that. Selling this hotel wouldn't be good for any of us."

Sell the hotel? Theodore felt his knees go weak. Selling this hotel would be disastrous for his family and all the other mice that lived and worked there. He and Lila and Cynthia would have to put a stop to all the bad publicity.

Theodore checked his watch. It was almost time for coffee break—time for Cynthia to show him the note she'd written.

Grandfather came to relieve him. "How's it going, Theodore?"

"O-o-okay," Theodore stuttered, unsure how to answer. If he couldn't find the culprit causing trouble, they might all be out in the alley.

Theodore hurried into the crowded cafeteria, searching for Cynthia. Lila caught his eye, but Cynthia was nowhere to be found. At his signal, Lila got up and walked out of the room. Theodore waited a moment and then followed her to the small conference room. He opened the door to the room and gaped at the mess inside.

Lila rushed forward. "My stars! What happened?"

Cynthia was sprawled facedown at the table. The notepaper in front of her was empty of words.

Lila shook her. "Cynthia, wake up! Wake up!"

Cynthia opened her eyes and blinked at them, confused. "Wha ... happened?"

"Look," said Theodore. "She's been hurt."

A bump welled out from the back of Cynthia's furry head. She raised a paw to it. "Ouch!"

"Who hit you?" Lila clasped her paws, looking around nervously.

"I don't know," wailed Cynthia. "I saw a shadow coming at me. That's all I remember."

Theodore's lips thinned with anger. "No humans could fit in this tiny room. It has to have been another mouse."

"But why would a mouse go after Cynthia?" asked Lila.

Theodore's thoughts whirled. Had someone found out about their secret investigation? But why would a mouse care? They'd want to be able to stay in the hotel too. No one wanted to end up in the alley. There had to be another reason for such an attack, but he couldn't think of any.

Cynthia's eyes rounded. "If we continue our investigation, maybe all of us will be in danger."

"We're in danger if we don't," said Theodore, his expression grim. "I overheard the GM talking. If there are any more bad reports of people getting sick or poisoned at the hotel, it might be sold out from under us."

"Oh, no!" said Lila. "Where would everyone go?"

"We'd all be out on the streets. And you know how dangerous that can be."

At the enormity of the problem, silence filled the room. No matter what danger they might be in, their detective work had to continue.

CHAPTER TEN

After making sure Cynthia was all right, Theodore left Lila guarding the door to the conference room. The note was important, and Cynthia, with her small paws, would need time to safely write it.

Grandfather was checking his watch as Theodore raced up to him at the doorman's post. He nodded and smiled when Theodore went right to work by bobbing his head to a new guest and saying, "Welcome to The Winston, sir."

The brown loafers swept by him. Theodore waited, but no mouse followed those shoes.

"It's been a slow morning," sighed Grandfather. "That's not good."

Theodore hesitated, then blurted out, "The hotel might be sold, Grandfather!"

"What? What are you talking about?"

Theodore took a deep breath to calm his racing heart. "I overheard the GM talking about it. If they get more bad publicity with stars being sick, the owners may have to sell the hotel."

Grandfather shook his head back and forth with dismay. "That would be horrible. Simply horrible."

Theodore blinked away a threatening tear. "Where would we go, Grandfather? What would happen to all my brothers and sisters? How would I be able to help Mama?"

Grandfather placed a paw on Theodore's shoulder. "Let's take it one day at a time. Let's make sure none of the humans sees us—not when a mouse arrives or leaves or any time in between. Understand? It's more important now than ever."

Theodore nodded. His stomach clenched. Getting the note to Simone would be difficult at best. But with the threat of the hotel being closed, he'd have to make sure it was done very, very carefully.

For the rest of the day, Theodore felt as if he'd swallowed a huge hunk of rotten cheese. He couldn't tell his Grandfather or anyone else what he, Lila, and Cynthia were doing, especially now when he knew a mouse, not a human, had hurt Cynthia, and they still didn't know why.

After work, Theodore snuck his way to the conference room and softly knocked on the door.

"Theodore?" whispered Lila from the other side of the wooden door.

"Yes, it's me. Open up!"

Lila open the door a crack. "C'mon in. The note is ready! Take a look!"

Theodore went over to the table and read:

We know what yur up to, Simone! Stop it! Evel deeds will not get you the role in the muvie!

Theodore sighed. Apparently Cynthia was a better writer than speller. However, they'd have to use the note as it was; the pressure to find the killer was too great for them to take the time to write another.

"We changed the wording a bit. We thought it sounded more threatening this way. What do you think?" said Lila.

"I think we'd better be very careful about delivering this note. Grandfather said it was more important than ever that none of us mice are seen in or around the hotel."

"Fine, but let's get something to eat first," said Cynthia. "I'm hungry."

They left the conference room, locking the door behind them.

"Remember, we each go separate ways so no one will see us together," warned Theodore. He waited until Lila and Cynthia were situated inside the cafeteria. Then he strolled into it as if he didn't have a care in the world. When he noticed Bandit seated at Lila's table, talking to her, Theodore's heart sank.

Cynthia was sitting at a table with the elderly female mouse he'd helped inside earlier in the week. He was headed in their direction when one of his sisters dashed over to him.

"Will you come sit with us?" She looked up at him with shining eyes.

"Sure." Theodore smiled at her. His family was the reason he was at The Winston. No matter what else was going on in his life, he'd always try his best to take care of them and to make them happy.

After forcing food into his whirling stomach, Theodore pushed away from the table.

"Off on another secret mission of yours, Theodore?" His mother gave him a teasing smile.

Theodore blinked in surprise. How did she know?

She waved a paw. "I'm just teasing you."

Theodore played along. "Yes! I'm off to save the world."

She laughed. "Have fun!"

Theodore hurried away, relieved his mother had no idea what he was up to.

When Theodore arrived at the conference room, Lila and Cynthia were busy, folding the note into a small rectangle.

"We thought this would make it easier for you to carry," said Cynthia. "I'll go first to make sure the coast is clear."

Theodore hefted the note in his arms and followed her out the door. The three of them hurried behind the hotel walls. In the plumbing system, it took the three of them to push, pull, and shove the note along the outside of the pipes leading to Simone's room. Theodore worried about what would happen when they got there. He and Lila had been caught unawares by one of the hotel maids checking rooms. If that happened again, it might ruin everything.

Outside the walls of Simone's room, the three of them came to an abrupt stop.

Cynthia faced Theodore with a wrinkled brow. "I don't see any of the usual cracks or open spaces between the floor and walls. How are we going to get inside?"

"What'll we do?" Lila shot Theodore a worried look.

"Wait here," Theodore said. "I'll check the pipes leading into the bathroom."

He set down the note and crawled up onto the pipes that went into the bathroom. What he had thought was an opening appeared to be a space filled with a soft white substance, an insulation of some kind. Theodore pushed against it and felt it give. After much work, he was able to push most of it aside.

He turned back to the others. "Okay, I think we can get through the wall. Hand me the note."

"I can't lift it," said Lila.

"Oh, for heaven's sake," grumped Cynthia. "Give it to me."

She held it up for a few seconds then dropped it with a groan.

"Quick! Grab it," squeaked Theodore. "It's starting to fall down through the pipes."

Lila and Cynthia each snatched a corner of the folded paper. Theodore rushed over to them and managed to lift it out of their arms.

"You sure are strong," gushed Lila, fluttering her long eyelashes at him.

Warm pride filled Theodore. He hoisted the note even higher. "Follow me."

He led Lila and Cynthia up the pipe, managed to push the note through the hole, and then helped them inside Simone's room.

"This isn't nearly as fancy as Juliet's bathroom," said Cynthia, glancing around with a look of disdain.

Lila frowned. "It's beautiful just the same."

"No bickering, remember?" said Theodore. "Take a careful look around. It's the humans' usual dinner hour. We need to make sure Simone and her dog are gone."

Leaving the note on the floor of the bathroom, the three of them crept to the door and peered out.

All was quiet.

"Where should we leave the note?" Lila's voice quavered with nervous excitement.

"Let me scout around." Theodore scurried into the room. The bedspread for the king bed was folded and placed on the ottoman at the end of the bed. A chocolate candy was perched on each pressed pillowcase. He smiled. The maid had come and gone for the nightly turndown service. They shouldn't be interrupted.

He went back to the bathroom and lifted the note. "Let's put it on the pillows, next to the chocolates. She won't miss it there."

Lila and Cynthia took one end of the note. He took the other. They scampered up the bedspread and onto the bed, moving as quickly as they could.

"Mmm, that chocolate smells yummy. Could I just take a tiny nibble?" said Lila.

Theodore whipped around. "No way. A good detective

leaves no evidence behind."

"Oh, yeah, that's right," said Lila. "I forgot."

Careful not to rip the paper, they unfolded the note, spreading the words across the pillow.

"There," said Theodore. "Now let's get out of here."

They scurried down the bedding, landing on the floor with three tiny thuds, just as the door to the room opened.

A flash of white fur charged their way.

"The dog!" gasped Lila.

CHAPTER ELEVEN

Frantically searching for a place to hide, Theodore grabbed Lila's arm and guided Cynthia ahead of him, encouraging her to hurry. They squeezed through the narrow space beneath the nightstand drawers next to the bed and huddled together, as far away from the edges as possible.

Fifi barked and pushed her nose under the nightstand as far as it would go. Her nostrils quivered at their smell.

Staring at the black tip of the dog's nose so close to them, Theodore's body turned cold. This dog was as persistent as the alley cat that had killed his father.

"Theodore, what are we going to do?" wailed Lila.

"We can't make a run for it," said Cynthia. "We can't be seen." Behind her glasses, her eyes blinked in nervous tics.

Theodore's mind raced. "I've got an idea. Listen up."

The next time Fifi stuck her nose under the bedside table, the three of them pounced on it with all their strength.

"Yowl!" Fifi let out a cry that brought Simone running over to her. "What's the matter? Did you bump your nose? Poor baby."

Fifi's howl turned into high-pitched yaps.

"Lose your tennis ball again? Naughty girl," Simone crooned. "Here. I'll try to reach it for you."

Theodore stared wide-eyed at Lila and Cynthia.

A hand with red painted nails appeared in the narrow space under the table and swiped Theodore off his feet.

"I almost got it!" Simone's fingers wiggled, reaching for him.

Theodore held in a squeak and scuttled out of the way.

Simone's hand swept the area once more.

Theodore, Lila and Cynthia scampered to the back wall, where they huddled together, shaking so hard Theodore feared the table might wobble.

Fifi's black nose appeared beside them.

"Look out!" Lila cried. She gathered the skirt of her dress and made a dash for the other side of the narrow space. Theodore and Lila caught up with her.

"My heart's pounding," gasped Lila. She placed a shaking paw upon her chest.

"How are we going to get out of here?" Cynthia's hysterical squeaking could barely be heard above Fifi's barking.

A knock at the door brought a sudden silence.

"Now what?" Simone groaned. Her hand disappeared from beneath the table.

Fifi barked and stuck her nose beneath the nightstand.

Taking a deep breath, Theodore swung his foot back and kicked Fifi's nose as hard as he could.

Fifi let out a yelp and began barking again.

"That's exactly what I mean," said a man's voice above the din. "You either have to silence the dog or place her in a kennel. She's disturbing everyone on the floor."

"Do you know who I am?" Simone's voice was shrill with indignation.

"Yes, Miss Skinner, I do," came the polite reply. "Might I suggest taking the dog for a walk? Perhaps that will calm her down."

"Wait until I tell the general manager how rude you've been to poor little Fifi and me," said Simone.

"I'm sure he'd like to hear from you," came the steady reply. Theodore smiled at the sarcasm in the man's voice.

"Well, I never!" pouted Simone. "Here, Fifi. Come."

"I'll walk you to the elevator," the man said. "I'm sure someone at the Concierge desk can direct you to the nearby dog park. It's a very popular spot."

"Fifi, stop barking and come here." Simone's voice turned shrill again.

From his place beneath the nightstand, Theodore watched Simone grab the dog and leave the room, slamming the door behind her. He turned to Lila and Cynthia. "We'd better move fast."

"But I wanted to hear what Simone had to say about the note," whined Cynthia.

"She didn't even notice it." Lila's voice was full of disappointment.

"C'mon, hurry," said Theodore firmly. He knew when Simone finally read their note, she'd tell everyone. And that could only mean more trouble.

CHAPTER TWELVE

The moment Theodore walked into the cafeteria, he knew something was wrong. A crowd had formed around Cynthia. She was showing everyone the bump on her head.

"I know one of you did that to me. My friends and I are going to find out who you are, and then you'll be sorry." She glanced over at Theodore. "Right, Theodore?"

Inside, Theodore's stomach scrunched into a knot of dismay. *Didn't she realize a good detective never gives out his plan?* "I don't know what you're talking about, Cynthia. I'm just the doorman, remember?" He gave her a stern look and walked away. Now, to find the culprit who'd attacked Cynthia, he'd have to change his strategy.

"What's she talking about?" asked one of his brothers when he sat down with his family. The mousekin's eyes glowed with excitement.

Theodore glanced at his mother and shrugged. "I don't have time to worry about it. I have to eat quickly and get to work." But he'd already made up his mind to do some interviewing during coffee break.

As the general manager had predicted, traffic in and out of the hotel slowed. On good days, Theodore barely had time to straighten after one bow before beginning another. Today, with so few arrivals and departures, he was bored.

When his coffee break came, Theodore hurried into the hotel, hoping to find Lila in the cafeteria. She was a late riser who usually ate breakfast mid-morning, but she was nowhere to be found.

On an impulse, he decided to go to Zanna's room. Maybe

Lila would be there. He waited until the coast was clear and then slipped into the shadows of the plumbing network. Up, up, up he climbed. Theodore had just entered Zanna's closet when he heard loud voices. He edged toward the door. A paw on his shoulder made him jump. He whipped around.

"Yo, bro," said Bandit.

"What are *you* doing here?" squeaked Theodore. His heart was still stuttering at the shock Bandit had given him.

Bandit held a finger to his lips. "Sssh. Listen."

"Don't try to deny it," screamed Simone. "It had to be you! You can't even spell!"

Theodore peeked outside the closet. Simone was waving a note in her hand in front of Zanna's face.

Zanna snatched the note out of Simone's hand and stared down at it. Her cheeks were pink with anger as she turned to Simone. "I did NOT write this note, and for your information, I can spell very well. Whoever wrote this note must have had a good reason to give it to you." Zanna's eyes narrowed. "Are you the one who gave me those sleeping pills? And what about Juliet? Did you try to do something to her?"

Holding up her hands, Simone backed away. "No, honest! It wasn't me! I don't know what you're talking about."

Zanna shook a finger at her. "I know how much you want the role of Gloria in the movie. You'd do anything for it, wouldn't you?"

Simone shook her head. "Not that way. No."

A knock came at the door.

Sam Horner entered the room, along with Rocky Strong.

"What's going on here?" said Sam. "I can hear the two of you battling all the way down the hall."

Tears rolled down Simone's cheeks. "Zanna is being awful to me, Sam. Just awful!" She sobbed into her hands.

"She's really good, huh," scoffed Bandit, standing beside Theodore. "She deserves an award for this performance."

Theodore nodded. He'd never seen tears form so fast.

Lila entered the closet and hurried over to them. "I was spying on the general manager, and ..." she took a deep breath "... and he was packing up some things in his office. It can't be a good sign."

Theodore shook his head. "No, that's not good at all."

"What's going on?" asked Bandit.

"Business at the hotel is slowing down," said Theodore. "And if it becomes too slow, the owners might close it down."

"Bummer. That would ruin things for us, huh?" Bandit shook his head.

Lila tugged on Theodore's shirtsleeve and nodded toward the humans. "Listen!"

"C'mon, Zanna," said Rocky. "Take my hand. Let's you and me get some fresh air."

After the door to the room had closed with a bang, Sam began talking. "Simone, now that Rocky and Zanna have left the room, listen to me. I know you want the starring role in this movie. That's probably not going to happen, but don't worry, I'll give you the starring role in my next movie. It's even a better role than this one. Trust me."

Shocked, Theodore edged closer to the closet entrance and peered out.

Simone's lips formed a perfect pout. "Oh, all right, I'll play along with you. But this idea of all of us staying here and becoming friends is ridiculous. We hate each other. See you later, Sam. I need to go lie down after the fuss with Zanna. It upset me so."

Lila came up beside Theodore. "Simone is very self-centered. Stupid, too."

Theodore gave her a questioning look, but Lila ignored it.

Simone left the room, and Sam plopped down on the couch. "I don't know how I ever got into this mess," he grumbled aloud. "I've invested too much money in this film to stop now. It better work out, or I'll be broke."

During the talk that followed, Theodore checked his watch and let out a gasp.

He was late! Very late!

CHAPTER THIRTEEN

"Please, Grandfather! You don't understand! I'm working on something that is very important to all of us mice!"

Grandfather shook a finger at him. "I warned you about being tardy, Theodore. I have no choice but to let you go. Beau Beady is next in line. He deserves a chance to do a better job than you."

Tears stung Theodore's eyes, but he blinked them away. His shoulders slumped. Somehow he'd get his job back. He had to, or his family would be kicked out of the hotel.

Beau Beady appeared wearing the uniform of a doorman. He gave Theodore a sharp, triumphant look that felt like a dagger entering Theodore's heart.

Grandfather put a hand on Theodore's shoulder. "I'm sorry, but I have to be fair with everyone, and you were twenty-nine minutes late. Please turn in your uniform."

Theodore wished he could tell Grandfather about his detective work, but even that might not help. His grandfather didn't approve of any mouse in the human part of the hotel or of their having anything to do with human guests. He'd tell Theodore it was too dangerous. Theodore let out a sigh. He couldn't tell anyone what he was doing until he discovered who was hurting the humans and who had attacked Cynthia.

At home, Theodore took off his uniform and pulled on a pair of jeans and a sweater. It pained him to see his uniform hanging limply on a hangar, ready to be turned in.

"Did you come home early to play with me?" asked his little brother, Sam. He looked up at Theodore wide-eyed, twitching his whiskers hopefully.

Theodore shook his head.

"Why aren't you at work, Theodore?" his mother asked, coming over to him. A worried look spread across her furry face.

Theodore hung his head.

"Was there a problem?" she asked gently.

Theodore nodded. "I was twenty-nine minutes late after coffee break."

"That's not like you," said his mother. "What happened?"

"I can't talk about it. Not yet."

Theodore's mother gazed at him. "Okay, son. When you're ready to discuss it, let me know. In the meantime, I'll have to figure out how to feed the family."

Guilt ate at Theodore. He left his home determined to do more detective work. And he really, really wished his replacement was anyone but Beau. They'd never gotten along. The memory of Beau's beady eyes shining with glee at Theodore's dismissal ate at Theodore's insides. Searching for Lila, he entered the cafeteria. At the sight of her empty table, he headed for the wall of plumbing and scurried up the pipes to Zanna's room.

He poked his head through the opening into Zanna's closet and blinked in surprise. Bandit was standing next to Lila at the entrance to the closet, and he had his arm around her.

"It's so romantic," sighed Lila.

"Yeah, it's like perfecto," said Bandit, pulling her closer.

Theodore gulped. Lila and Bandit were definitely romantically involved. Disappointment speared him. He was about to leave when Bandit noticed him.

"Yo, Ted! What are you doing here?"

"Well, I ... I ..." Theodore stammered.

"Your uniform! Why aren't you wearing it?" asked Lila.

"I lost my job," Theodore reluctantly admitted.

"You mean you're *nothing* now?" Lila said.

Theodore's cheeks turned fiery hot. He struggled for something to say, but his throat had closed with pain.

Lila hurried over to him. "I'm sorry. I didn't mean that the way it sounded."

Theodore nodded, but inside him, hurt strummed his heartstrings. Lila was lost to him forever. She was right. He was nothing. He couldn't even say he was just the doorman anymore.

Bandit eyed him. "So, what'cha doin' up here?"

Theodore tried to focus on the problem that faced all of them. If he didn't solve the mystery behind the attempted murders, it wouldn't matter to him or anyone else if he was a doorman at The Winston. It would be closed down.

"I need to talk to everyone about ..."

"Sshh!" said Lila. "Listen!"

Theodore crept to the opening in the closet door and peered out. Rocky and Zanna were sitting and facing each other on the couch.

"I love you, Zanna! Will you marry me?" Rocky's words held a tenderness Theodore recognized as true love.

Zanna's voice was soft with affection. "Yes, Rocky! I will! I will! But not until after the film is done."

Lila turned to them, her hands clasped. Her sweet pink eyes grew teary. "I'm so happy I could cry."

Zanna spoke up again. "For now, Rocky, no one must know about us, especially Simone. You know how she feels about you and me together."

"Do you love me?" Rocky asked.

She nodded, and Rocky kissed her.

"Let's get out of here. It's way too mushy in there," said

Bandit, sticking a finger down his throat.

"Oh, but it's so sweet," gushed Lila.

Theodore cringed at the adoring look she gave Bandit and cleared his throat. "I need to talk to both of you. Follow me."

The three of them scampered down to the conference room. Bandit leaned back in one of the chairs around the table. "Yeah? So what's on your mind, Ted?"

"Is it something about the mystery?" asked Lila.

Bandit looked sharply from Lila to Theodore. "What mystery? What are you talking about?"

Lila nodded to Theodore. "Go ahead, tell him."

"Someone has been making the stars sick. We think it might be attempted murder."

Bandit started to laugh.

"Why are you doing that?" Lila asked, wide-eyed.

Theodore clenched his paws. "What's so funny? They might shut down the hotel, and then we'll all be out in the alley. The Winston gives us a decent place to live and work. Without it, where would we be?"

Bandit's laughter came to an abrupt stop. His expression turned serious. "Like, man, I didn't know anything about The Winston shutting down. I wasn't trying to kill anyone, just make 'em sick. That's all."

Theodore's legs folded. He plopped down in a chair opposite Bandit. "You're the one who made Juliet and Zanna sick?"

Lila put her fists on her hips and glared at Bandit. "Just what did you do to her?"

Bandit held up a paw in defense. "Whoa! I didn't say anything about Zanna! Why would I want to harm her? My human loves her. You heard him. He asked her to marry him!"

Theodore glared at him. "You'd better tell us exactly

what's going on, Bandit! This is serious."

"Okay, Ted. Here's how it is. You know how pushy Juliet is, right? I overheard her and Sam talking. Sam was about to give in to her demands that she be given the starring role opposite Rocky. He even set up a television interview for her. I couldn't let that happen. Right, Lila?"

Lila was in on it? Theodore turned to her. Her white furry cheeks were highlighted in bright red. "You knew about this?"

"No, no, no. I told Bandit how much Zanna liked Rocky and how I hoped they'd get together. I even ..."

Theodore turned away from her, not even letting her finish. It was one more instance of Lila and Bandit being a team and leaving him out. "Go on, Bandit. Tell me the rest."

"See, it's like I had to do something. Rocky got real mad when he found out Juliet might take Zanna's place. He said it might mean the end of his career because no one would believe he was in love with Juliet, that even he couldn't act *that* well."

"So what did you do? Poison Juliet?" Theodore could barely keep his temper in control.

"Yo, man! I didn't poison her! I just put a little Ipecac in her sleeping pills. That stuff doesn't kill you; it just makes you throw up."

Lila clasped her cheeks with her paws. "Oh, no! I wanted Zanna to be the star, but not like this."

Theodore narrowed his eyes at Bandit. "You say you did nothing to Zanna, but why did you attack Cynthia?"

Bandit's jaw dropped. "Whoa! I so did not do that! Why would I?"

"Someone knocked her out. We have to find answers or we may all be out on the street."

"What about Maurice?" said Bandit. "There might be a

whole lot more to him than a round belly."

Theodore nodded thoughtfully. Maurice seemed harmless, but detectives knew that sometimes the people who seemed the most innocent were the ones who did all the dirty deeds.

"Let's go find him," said Lila.

Theodore shook his head. "You stay here with Bandit. I'll go by myself."

Lila's adorable pink eyes showed her hurt. "Are you trying to get rid of me?"

"No, uh, yeah, I thought the two of you might want to be alone," stammered Theodore, surprised by her reaction.

"Alone with Bandit? No way. I'm going with you and that's that," Lila announced. "We detectives have to stick together."

Bandit waved them away. "See you later. I've got something I have to do."

"You'd better not be up to any more trouble," warned Theodore. "C'mon, Lila, we have to hurry. It's almost lunch time, and I want to speak to Maurice before then."

Theodore headed up the pipes.

"Do you know where we're going?" asked Lila, hurrying to keep pace with him.

Theodore nodded. "Sam Horner is next door to Juliet. That's where Maurice probably is." He scampered through the tangle of pipes as fast as he could. Catching suspects off guard was sometimes how detectives got confessions.

When they reached the outside of Sam's room, Theodore pointed to a large round hole. "Look! Maurice has made it easy for us."

Theodore entered the hole and found himself in the living room of Sam's suite. Lila came up behind him. "Wow! This is even bigger than Juliet's suite!"

A dining room table set with two place settings sat at one end of the room. Above it, hung a crystal chandelier. The glass dangling from the fixture sparkled in the sunlight that shone through the sliding glass doors that led to a balcony along the length of the room. Rainbows formed by the crystals danced in the air. Theodore sucked in his breath. It was beautiful.

Lila poked Theodore in the ribs. "There he is." She pointed an accusing finger to the shadow beneath the table. Maurice was busy, gobbling up what Theodore suspected were the last of the crumbs from a late breakfast.

Theodore held a finger to his lips, prepared to spring a surprise. But Lila was already marching toward Maurice, waving a finger at him. "All right, we've got you now."

Theodore rolled his eyes and hurried to catch up to her before she ruined everything.

"What are you two doing here?" asked Maurice, licking a crumb from his lips. "This is private property. My human doesn't like it when anyone else is here."

"Then why are there two place settings at the table?" scoffed Theodore. "Does he eat two meals at a time?" A good detective noticed things like that.

Maurice's expression turned sheepish. "He had a breakfast meeting. So what?"

Theodore worked to keep calm under Maurice's scornful stare. "Look, we're not here to talk about Sam; we're here to talk to you."

Maurice's eyes widened. "Me? Why? I didn't do anything."

"We think you did," said Lila.

Theodore held up his hand. "Please, Lila. Let me explain to Maurice exactly what's going on." He proceeded to tell Maurice about the general manager's concern about the owners' threat to close the hotel if business did not pick up. "He's blaming it on the bad press the hotel is getting because two famous stars have taken ill. The hotel food is being blamed for it."

Maurice patted his stomach. "There's nothing wrong with the hotel food. It's among the best."

"We know that," said Lila. "We've already found out..."

Theodore had to shut Lila up before she ruined this investigation. He stomped on her tail.

"SQUEEEEK!" She whipped around, holding onto her tail. "Why did you do that?"

Theodore ignored the glare she gave him and continued. "So, Maurice, we're talking to all the mice in the building to find out what they might have heard or seen about Zanna and Juliet getting sick. Any reason at all to think that someone might have poisoned them?"

Theodore kept his voice light though he'd already noticed the way Maurice's eyes had shifted away from him.

"We ..." Lila began and stopped again when Theodore lifted his foot.

"We believe Zanna might have been given sleeping pills. Know anything about it?"

Maurice slowly nodded his head. "You'd better talk to Bandit. I'm pretty sure he's involved in something nefarious. I'm positive he had something to do with Juliet being sick."

"We ..." Lila began and stopped when Theodore glared at her.

"We'll speak to him about it," said Theodore. "But, what about you?"

"Me? Well, I ... Well, I ..."

Lila stomped her foot. "Just tell us!"

Maurice sank down onto the Oriental rug and gazed up at them with a worried expression. "Well, it was like this. Zanna came in here demanding that Sam stop teasing her about the role in the movie. She either got it or she didn't. And if she didn't get it, Rocky promised to leave with her. I had to let her know that my human shouldn't be treated that way. She was a nobody until Sam put her in a movie and made her a star. It was a warning. That's all."

Theodore blinked with surprise.

Lila placed her paws on her hips and faced Maurice. "My Zanna is a bigger star than Sam Horner could ever make her. Don't forget it."

"Star or not, she's got to cooperate. If Sam doesn't get this film made, it's over for him. Then where will I be?"

"Out on the street with the rest of us. This foolishness has to stop," said Theodore in clipping words. He was as angry as he'd ever been. "And by the way, what were you doing in the conference room the other day?"

"Huh? Conference room? I don't know what you're talking about. Why would I go there? Food is served in the cafeteria."

"Okay. No more trouble from you. Is that clear?"

Maurice nodded. "Sorry. I was just trying to help my human out."

"Help yourself, don't you mean?" snapped Lila. "No wonder there's never any scraps left in the hotel suites for the rest of us. You eat them all. You're supposed to share with the rest of us. C'mon, Theodore. Let's go."

Just before Theodore slipped through the hole to leave, he turned around. Maurice was busily searching for scraps as if nothing bad had ever happened.

Lila's eyes shone. "We're a great detective team, huh? Did you see how easily I made him talk?"

Theodore couldn't stop the grin that spread across his face. When Lila's face lit up like that she was ... well, totally adorable.

"Now that we know there's no real killer here at the hotel, the investigation is over. Right, Theodore?"

Theodore shook his head. "Don't forget the culprit who hit Cynthia. There's a bad mouse among us. That's a mystery of its own—a mystery I intend to solve."

Lila nodded. "Right. So we're still a team?" Her pink eyes pleaded with him.

Theodore sighed. "I guess so. But we have only two days left to find the guilty one."

CHAPTER FOURTEEN

Theodore headed back to the cafeteria with Lila. As he passed the entrance to the mouse hotel, he stopped and peered out at the doorman's post. Beau Beady glanced over at him and gave him a triumphant grin. Theodore's stomach curled. Beau was so busy showing off he didn't even notice the grandmotherly mouse Theodore had helped inside earlier. Now, without Beau's help, she teetered onto the sidewalk alone.

"What do you want, Theodore?" said Beau. "No loitering around the entrance. You know the rules."

Theodore knew the rules all right, and they didn't include being nasty to the other mice.

"I don't think the new doorman is very nice," huffed Lila as they went on their way. "He acts like he owns the place."

Theodore nodded, but could say nothing. He'd lost his job fair and square. The doorman was expected to be at his post according to his schedule, and he'd failed miserably. If he hadn't been caught up in solving mysteries, he'd still have his job, and his family would be safe.

Theodore and Lila entered the cafeteria to find it abuzz with conversation.

Bandit quickly joined them.

"What's happening?" asked Lila.

"It's the Producer. They had to call an ambulance for him. Food poisoning. Everyone is upset. A meeting of all the mice has been called."

The cafeteria began filling. Even Beau Beady found a place in the crowd.

One of Theodore's sisters rushed up to him. "Is it true, Theodore? Are we going to get kicked out of here?" A tear trickled down her furry cheek. "Where are we going to live? What will we do?"

Theodore gave her a quick hug. "Don't worry! We'll find a way to end all this confusion."

She looked up at him with adoring eyes. "I knew you would help us."

Theodore drummed up an encouraging smile, but inside he wondered how the hotel could survive this latest blow.

Lila tugged on his arm and gave him a worried look. "Theodore, you've got to do something! Everyone's in a panic."

Theodore jumped up on a chair. "Attention, everybody! We are not about to kicked out of the hotel just yet! Instead of talk of packing up your belongings, we should be discussing ways to help the hotel."

"Yeah?" Beau said with a sneer, brushing a speck of dust off his uniform. "Just what are you planning to do, Theodore? You're not even the doorman anymore."

"Right!" came another cry. "We're just mice. How can we stop the humans from fighting and making a mess of things?"

"It isn't just the humans ..."began Lila.

Theodore glared at her.

Lila glanced at him, covered her mouth with her paws, and remained silent.

Theodore didn't want anyone to know there was a bad mouse among them, someone willing to interfere with his investigation—an investigation meant to save the hotel. Lila was the cutest mouse he'd ever seen, but without a doubt, she was the worst detective ever!

Theodore cleared his throat. "Everyone needs to remain

calm. I've been looking into this matter and I feel it's important to carry on with our duties. However, under no circumstances should any of us be seen by the humans. Another investigation of the hotel kitchen is sure to follow this latest development."

"Why should we listen to you, Theodore?" challenged Beau.

Grandfather walked up next to the chair and faced the crowd. "Theodore may no longer be the doorman but he's always shown a rare sense of responsibility. Look how he's helped keep his family together. He has no reason to mislead us. Right, Theodore?"

Theodore nodded, but now he had two mysteries to solve, and time was running out. His mind whirled as he stepped down off the chair. Bandit and Maurice had admitted to making Juliet and Zanna sick. Who wanted Sam Horner out of the way? And who had hurt Cynthia?

Theodore was pretty sure neither Lila nor Cynthia would be after Sam. And Maurice was too busy finding crumbs to get into too much trouble. So who could it be? Earlier Bandit had left him, saying he had to take care of something. Had he meant poisoning Sam?

Bandit approached him, flung an arm around Lila, and said, "C'mon. Let's get out of here."

Fighting a stab of despair at the smile on Lila's face, Theodore watched them walk away.

Theodore's mother approached him. "Are you okay, son? You look upset."

He shrugged. He couldn't tell anyone, especially his mother, how he felt about Lila.

She patted his back. "Remember, you're not to mingle with the guest mice. We are just part of the hotel staff."

Hotel staff? He didn't even have a job anymore. He hung

his head. He had nothing to offer anyone.

Grandfather had once told Theodore when he felt bad about himself, it was time to think of helping others. Dragging himself out of his misery at being a "nobody", Theodore headed up to Sam Horner's set of rooms.

He easily crawled through the round hole Maurice had made, entered the living area of the Producer's suite, and came to a quick stop. A loud raspy noise filled the air in noisy waves. It took a moment for Theodore to realize it was the sound of snoring.

He entered the room on tiptoe and glanced around. The sound was coming from the dining room table.

Theodore raced over to the table, up one of its wooden carved legs, and let out a sigh. Maurice lay on his back in the middle of a large platter of cold meats and cheeses. With each snorting breath, Maurice's stomach rose and fell, up and down, like a beach ball riding tall ocean waves.

Avoiding several platters of food and a large tureen of soup, Theodore hurried over to Maurice and shook him none too gently. "Wake up! Wake up! You're putting the rest of us in danger!"

Maurice opened his eyes and gave Theodore a blank look. "Huh?"

"Get up right now! We need to get out of here before some human sees us!"

Theodore tugged on Maurice's arm, but he sank back down on the plate, almost pulling Theodore on top of him.

The sound of someone at the door made Theodore's pulse pound. "C'mon!" He grabbed hold of Maurice's paws, yanked him upright, and pushed him to the edge of the table. "Jump, Maurice!"

"I can't ..." Maurice started to say, and went flying through the air. He landed with a thump on the soft carpet beside Theodore. "Why'd you do that?"

"Room Service! Is anyone here?" came the call from the doorway.

Theodore clutched one of Maurice's paws and took off.

"I can't ... move ... that fast ..." Maurice's breath came out in gasps as they sprinted across the room.

They'd almost reached the hole in the wall when they

heard a shout.

"Look here!"

Theodore's heart stuttered. He turned to find two servers from the kitchen inspecting the table.

"If I'm not mistaken, those are little paw prints," muttered the male server. He squinted at the white tablecloth.

"Paw prints? At The Winston Hotel? Impossible!" said the woman with him.

"I'm not so sure ..." the man said. "We'd better take a good look around."

Theodore pushed Maurice into the hole in the baseboard and slid in behind him. As he peeked at the humans from inside the hole, Theodore's mouth turned dry. If it was discovered mice had actually been in the Presidential Suite of all places, they wouldn't even have time to pack their things before being attacked by exterminators.

"We can't take the time to go looking for trouble," the woman said. "The hotel is cutting down on staff, and if we don't do our job and leave here in a hurry, we might be next."

The man nodded. "You're right. Let's clean up this mess and return to the kitchen. We have to help serve a banquet."

Theodore clasped his paws in prayerful thanks and turned back to Maurice, who was slumped against one of the pipes behind the wall. Anger rose in Theodore all over again. He shook a finger at Maurice.

"If I hadn't happened to come along when I did, you might have been discovered. Any idea how many other lives would have been destroyed by that?"

Maurice's tan cheeks turned dark. "I'm sorry. Honest. It's just that I hate to see food go to waste. Know what I mean?"

Theodore sighed. It would go to waste all right—Maurice's waist. "I need the truth, Maurice. Did you poison the Producer?"

Maurice's mouth rounded. "Me? Why would I poison Sam? No, no. It's not what you think. It was poisoning all right. Food poisoning. Sam is allergic to brussel sprouts. I tried to warn him brussel sprouts were in the soup, but even though I squeaked and squeaked, he paid no attention to me."

Theodore narrowed his eyes at Maurice. "Is this the truth, the whole truth, and nothing but the truth?"

Maurice lifted a paw and nodded. "It's happened before. He'll be back in a day or so."

"A day or so?" Theodore could hardly swallow. Would that bit of bad press mean the end of the hotel? There was only one way to find out.

He turned to Maurice. "From here on in, you stay in the mouse section of the hotel. Understand?"

Maurice nodded meekly. "I'm sorry. I really am. I'll try to do better. I promise."

"Do me a favor," said Theodore. "Go down to the cafeteria, find Lila, and tell her what you told me."

"Where are you going?"

"On a mission of my own."

Dangerous as it was, Theodore had to find some answers.

CHAPTER FIFTEEN

Theodore waited until Maurice had scurried down the pipes before taking off on his own. Grateful for his dark clothes, he stayed to the shadows as he made his way down the long hallway to the GM's office. He heard angry voices from inside and huddled outside the door to listen.

"But, sir," came the familiar GM's voice. "I assure you, we're doing all we can to counter the bad press we've been getting."

Another voice, an angry one, shouted, "You were hired to increase business, not destroy it! As a representative of the investors, I'm here to warn you that not only are you about to lose your job, but now the hotel is in danger of being sold or closed."

"It's true that a few high-profile people have had bad experiences here, but ..." said the GM.

"I'm not listening to any excuses," interrupted the representative. "You'd better come up with a way to create good news for the hotel, or it's all over."

The door to the GM's office flew open beside Theodore with a bang. Highly polished black shoes marched by him.

Theodore pasted himself against the door frame, praying he wouldn't be noticed.

"Wait, sir!" cried the GM, chasing after the man.

Theodore took off in the opposite direction, running as fast as he could toward the stairway. A hidden access to the mouse hotel was just beyond it.

While the GM tried to smooth things over at the other end of the hall, Theodore slipped in behind the walls of the hotel.

He sat a moment, gasping for breath. His mind spun. *Good news for the hotel? What did the representative for the investors mean?*

Theodore suddenly understood.

He took off running.

Entering the cafeteria, he gazed around. Spying Cynthia, he hurried over to her. "I need you to do something for me."

Cynthia looked up at him, blinking rapidly behind her glasses. "Why should I help you? You're not even the doorman anymore."

Theodore pressed his lips together. If they didn't cooperate and work together, the hotel might soon close.

Lila came over to their table. "What's going on, Theodore? Maurice told me about the Producer's allergy to brussel sprouts."

Cynthia's eyes widened. "But I thought ..."

"Listen," said Theodore, unwilling to waste a moment. "I have a plan to save the hotel. But I need help from both of you. Come with me."

Theodore led them to the small conference room and opened the door. "Hurry inside. We've no time to lose."

In a matter of moments, Theodore filled them in on what he'd heard and what he wanted to do about it.

Lila clapped her hands. "Perfect! I think it will work. I'll get paper and pen from Zanna's room."

"I'll help you," said Theodore.

"And I'll stay here, composing the note," Cynthia said. "I don't think anyone is going to attack me again. And if they try, I'll be ready for them." She held up her fisted paws.

Theodore and Lila hurried up to Zanna's room and stood for a moment in the dim closet, assessing the situation.

"Good. All's quiet," murmured Theodore. "Let's go."

Lila grabbed his arm, holding him back. "You're a good

mouse, Theodore. No matter how this ends, I appreciate everything you've done for all of us." She stood on her toes and planted a kiss on his cheek.

Theodore's paw traveled to the spot where Lila had kissed him. It felt on fire. He couldn't think of a single thing to say. Lila liked him? Really liked him?

"Are you ready?" Lila finally asked.

Theodore nodded. He was ready all right—ready to fall completely in love with the little white mouse who had won his heart.

"Let's go," said Lila, snapping Theodore out of his trance.

They left the closet and entered the room, searching for the easiest, fastest way to retrieve a sheet of paper and a pen. Who knew when some human might come along?

"Over there," said Theodore, pointing to the desk in the corner. They raced over to it and scampered up one of its legs. Hotel stationery was neatly stacked in a cubby hole on the desk. Theodore tugged on the corner of one sheet. The whole stash scattered across the desk and fell onto the floor.

Lila tried to gather them together, but as she stretched her arms around a few, others tumbled and fell.

"Leave them," ordered Theodore. "Sounds like someone's at the door." He folded a sheet of paper in his paws and tucked it into his pants. "We have to get out of here.."

They'd just made their way to the floor when a maid entered the room, carrying a vacuum cleaner.

Theodore snatched Lila's arm and dragged her behind one of the legs of the desk. He closed his eyes and leaned against it, trembling all over.

"What is it?" Lila asked softly.

"The vacuum cleaner," Theodore managed to say. "A friend of mine ..." He couldn't go on. The memory of losing one of his best friends to that hungry machine was too much.

Understanding crossed Lila's face. She rubbed his back. "I'm so sorry."

Theodore quieted, grateful for her kindness. He tensed again when the maid walked over to the desk.

"Such slobs these movie people are," the maid muttered. "It's one mess after another."

Lila's eyes bulged with outrage. No one criticized her Zanna. She clamped fists on her hips and opened her mouth to protest.

Alarm rang inside Theodore. He had to do something to stop her squeaking, but what?

Without another thought, Theodore leaned over and kissed her on the mouth. And he didn't stop until the maid had picked up all the papers on the floor and moved away.

When Theodore pulled away from Lila, she stared at him wide-eyed. "That was ... that was ...

Theodore's body turned ice cold with dread. He glanced away and back again. "Awful?"

Lila's eyes glowed a delicate pink. "No, it was sweet. Very, very sweet."

Theodore's heart sped up. "You mean it?"

Lila gave him a shy smile and nodded.

Their tender moment was destroyed by the sound of the vacuum cleaner starting up.

"Run!" squeaked Theodore. He grabbed Lila's paw and scurried as fast as his legs could carry him.

Safe inside the closet, he caught his breath. "We'll have to find another way to get a pen."

"We can't stay here," agreed Lila. "We might be killed."

Theodore and Lila entered the conference room to find Cynthia sitting at the long table. She grinned and held up a large pen.

"Where did you get that?" asked Theodore, surprised but pleased.

"Over there. You ought to see all the stuff hidden away!" Cynthia led them to the closet and opened the door. Inside, it was packed with human things taken from The Winston—pens, washcloths, cups, glasses, even small plates, all with the hotel logo on them.

"Those are stolen goods," Theodore cried. "I wonder who hid them there."

Cynthia shrugged. "I don't know, but one of us is a thief."

"Maybe the mouse that put them there is the one that hit you over the head," suggested Lila.

Theodore grinned at her. Lila wasn't such a bad detective after all. "We'll keep a careful watch on who comes in and out of the conference room. In the meantime, we have to get this note written."

Cynthia gave him a smug smile. "I have it all figured out."

Theodore and Lila anxiously paced the room while Cynthia struggled with the pen, writing down the message they had to deliver. Each minute was precious. The movie stars were due to leave in another day.

CHAPTER SIXTEEN

There!" said Cynthia. "I'm done." She held up the note for them to see.

Zanna, how bout a weeding here at the hotel? It wood be loverly.

Her eyes shiny, Lila clasped her paws together. "It would be so romantic if Zanna had her wedding here at the hotel! This is where Rocky proposed to her."

"This has to work," said Theodore. "If it does, The Winston Hotel would once more be the place where everyone wants to go. Then, there would be no talk about closing it."

"C'mon! Let's take the note up to Zanna's room," said Lila. "I can't wait to hear what she says when she reads it."

Handling the note with extra care, the conspirators carried it up through the plumbing to Zanna's room. They inched the note through the hole into the closet and then followed it inside. All seemed quiet. The three of them crept to the half-open closet door and peered out.

"Ohhh," whispered Lila. "Rocky's here."

Zanna and Rocky were sitting on the couch. Rocky gave Zanna a kiss.

Theodore glanced at Lila, remembering how sweet their kiss had been. Lila smiled and looked away. He turned his attention back to the stars.

"I'd better be going," said Rocky, pulling away from Zanna. "Thanks for lunch. I have to get ready for a press interview."

"Mmm, stay for a few minutes more," pleaded Zanna, snuggling up against him.

Rocky laughed softly, and they kissed again.

Theodore snatched up the note and scampered across the room. Hopefully, the kiss would last long enough for him to place the note by the couch and get back to the closet without being seen.

He'd just unfolded the note on the carpet when Zanna sat up and said, "Guess I'd better not keep you any longer, Rocky." Her feet hit the carpet next to Theodore.

He held back a squeak and scurried beneath the couch.

"Oh!" said Zanna. "What's this?" Her hands reached down in front of Theodore and took hold of the note.

The tinkle of her laughter filled the air with soft music. "Look at this, Rocky! The maid must have left this for me. A wedding here at The Winston? It would be *loverly*, it says. Like my last name. Isn't that the cutest thing ever?"

"I like the whole idea," said Rocky. "We could get married this weekend."

"Silly," said Zanna playfully. "You know I need time to get ready."

"I'm serious, Zanna. Let's not have one of those long engagements. You've won my heart. Why don't we announce our engagement and wedding at the same time? You know how I hate to wait for things."

Theodore held his breath. He looked across the room. Lila had her fingers crossed. Cynthia raised her thumbs. This could be the hotel's lucky break.

After what seemed an eternity, Zanna said, "Let's do it! Call the GM and ask if he'll help us get it pulled together. I'll call my friends and give them a heads-up."

"Join me for the press conference, darling. I'll meet you there."

"Okay," said Zanna. "This is so-o-o exciting!"

Theodore gazed at Lila. She was standing beside Cynthia, her hands clasped, a dreamy expression on her furry face. He couldn't help smiling. She'd worn that same look after his kiss.

Rocky left, and while Zanna was busy on the phone, Theodore sprinted across the room to the closet.

"It's working!" cried Lila, hugging him and jumping up and down joyfully.

They rocked to a stop.

He grinned and turned to Cynthia. "Good job! Thanks!"

Cynthia gave him a coy look and put an arm around Lila. "I see the way you and Lila are looking at each other. Maybe we'll *all* have a wedding."

Theodore felt as if the air in his lungs had been punched out of him. He loved Lila, but he couldn't ask her to marry him. He wasn't even the doorman anymore.

Lila gazed up at him, her pink eyes aglow. He forgot about everything, but her. Maybe she would consider becoming his girlfriend. He gathered his courage to ask her.

"Lila?"

"Yes?" she squeaked.

"Will you ..."

"Yes, I'll marry you," she said before he could finish. She threw her arms around him. "I'm so happy!"

Lost in her embrace, his mind spinning, Theodore didn't have the heart to tell her he'd been about to say, "Will you wait for me?" He adored her, but how could he take care of her and his family too?

Theodore left Lila and Cynthia dancing with excitement and hurried down to the doorman's post. His job of hotel detective wasn't done.

Beau Beady was standing by the revolving door. "What do you want, Theodore?" he said with a sneer that hurt.

Theodore took a deep breath, trying to hold back a nasty reply. "I'm looking for my grandfather."

"As you can plainly see, he isn't here. So, you'd better go."

But Theodore had already noticed a number of people gathered in front of the hotel.

"No loitering," said Beau, elbowing Theodore.

Theodore stood his ground. If he wasn't mistaken, this is the announcement he'd been hoping for.

The GM's familiar brown shoes appeared and then his voice rang out. "Ladies and gentlemen of the press, I have an exciting announcement to make. As you know, several of the stars associated with Sam Horner's new upcoming movie have been staying here at The Winston. Two of the biggest stars, Zanna Loverly and Rocky Strong have not only fallen in love with the hotel, they've fallen in love with each other. And, I'm proud to say, they've chosen The Winston for their wedding and reception. In true Winston Hotel fashion, it will be the social event of the season, and it's all happening here in two days."

A barrage of questions filled the air. Theodore didn't wait around to listen to them. He had to find Grandfather. And fast!

Grandfather was sitting at a table in the cafeteria with the little old lady mouse Theodore had assisted into the hotel earlier. He hurried over to them.

" Excuse me, Grandfather, could I speak to you?"

Grandfather's eyes widened. He nodded toward the lady. "Slow down, boy, and please say hello to an old friend of mine. Lucinda, this is my grandson, Theodore."

Lucinda smiled. "Weren't you the doorman who helped

me inside?"

Theodore nodded. "I ... I ... was..."

"Theodore is no longer the doorman," Grandfather explained to Lucinda.

Her eyebrows arched like question marks. "Why ever not?"

Grandfather turned to Theodore with a stern look.

"I ... I ... I was late to my job," mumbled Theodore, feeling his heart sink. He turned to go.

"I'm sorry, Theodore. I really am," said Grandfather. "But rules are rules."

Disheartened, Theodore headed out of the cafeteria. What was he going to do now?

A tap on his shoulder stopped him. He turned to face Lucinda. Her wrinkled face couldn't hide the gleam in her eyes. "I think we may be able to work together, young man. Come sit with us a minute."

Theodore reluctantly took a seat beside Grandfather and faced Lucinda.

She smiled at him. "Your Grandfather told me how you have been helping your mother and brothers and sisters. I admire such loyalty and I must say, your replacement has been nothing but rude to everyone. It's time I told both of you what I suspect and why I'm here."

She leaned forward and spoke softly. "I'm here on a spying mission. There's someone in our midst that may be a danger to us all." She turned to Theodore. "I understand you're a detective extraordinaire. I'm going to need your help."

Detective extraordinaire? Pride filled Theodore. It felt so good to be recognized for something he did well. "Yes, Ma'am. I'm here to help you."

She smiled at him. "I have my suspicion as to who it is,

but I need to have proof."

Theodore nodded. He had a suspicion of his own.

"Okay, here's what I want you to do." She whispered into Theodore's ear.

He listened. By the time she was through, he was smiling. He and Lucinda were after the same culprit.

"Remember," said Lucinda, "you have to nab him in the act."

Theodore nodded. Prickles of excitement ran down his back. He'd catch the thief and save his family and others, including Lila, from being kicked out of the hotel.

As he left the table, Theodore brimmed with hope. Their plan just might work.

CHAPTER SEVENTEEN

Theodore entered the conference room and looked around. Empty. He spied the pen Cynthia had left on the table. He went over to it and pushed it down to the floor. Then he dragged the pen outside the room and taking care not to be seen, placed it on the carpet near the door. Giving the pen a little pat, he smiled. The trap was set.

He scurried back into the room and waited. If his suspicions were right, he'd soon have the hotel thief in his paws. He checked his watch. Coffee break time.

Theodore went over to the tall draperies by the windows, tucked himself behind them, and drew a deep breath.

A sound at the door soon caught his attention. He tensed. The stealthy tap, tap of paws against the wooden floor prompted Theodore to get ready. Hearing the scrape of the pen being dragged across the wooden floor, he smiled. The thief had taken the bait.

Still, he waited.

At the squeak of the closet door being opened, Theodore leapt out from behind the drapes. "Hah! I've caught you! You're the one stealing from the hotel!"

Beau's eyes widened with surprise. Then a nasty smirk distorted his features. "I'll tell everyone it was you, Theodore! No one will believe you."

"I think they will," Theodore retorted. "And I believe I've solved another mystery. You're the one who hit Cynthia over the head. You wanted to prevent her from seeing you hide more stolen goods. You're in trouble for more than stealing, Beau."

"Why would anyone trust your word against mine?" sneered Beau. "You're not even the doorman anymore."

The conference room door opened with a bang. "And neither are you," said Grandfather, marching inside the room with two security mice. "You've been stealing from the hotel, putting others at risk. Doing harm to any other mouse is a very serious thing."

The security mice stood on either side of Beau, looking very stern.

Beau shook a fist at Theodore. "It's all *your* fault. You ratted me out."

"No," came another voice. "I did."

"Great-aunt Lucinda?" Beau's eyes appeared to bulge from his head with surprise.

The old mouse walked into the room and leaned on her cane. Theodore went to her side.

"Thank you," she said to him. "You handled that well."

"He was working with you?" Beau shook his head. "I should've known."

Lucinda shook her cane at Beau. "You should've known not to steal. Your mother requested my assistance. She was sure you were up to your old tricks. You've shamed the family. Now, my boy, it's time to pay for your poor behavior. I've suggested that in addition to returning the items you've stolen and making an apology to Cynthia, you work on a cleanup project the Council has in mind. With an upcoming wedding, the place needs a little sprucing up."

"Wedding?" Beau wrinkled his nose. "What wedding?"

Lucinda smiled at Theodore. "We're all so excited about you and Lila. Everyone loves a wedding."

Theodore shuffled his feet, shyly. News certainly traveled fast in a hotel.

"Theodore and Lila?" gasped Beau.

"Yes. Theodore and Lila are getting married. That's why I'm assigning him the job of doorman again," announced Grandfather.

Theodore blinked in surprise. Things were turning out fine after all. He grinned at the news. Having his old job back was wonderful. He could support his family again. He could marry Lila after all.

Grandfather winked at him, and took hold of Lucinda's hand.

Maybe, thought Theodore, other weddings would take place in time. Grandfather sure looked happy.

Over the next few days, the Winston Hotel was abuzz with activity, both in the human area and behind the walls where the mice lived and worked. Like Lucinda said, everyone, it seemed, loved a wedding. All the mice were throwing themselves into the task of making his wedding memorable.

The ballroom next to the cafeteria was slowly being turned into a magical place with sparkling lights and bits and pieces of decorations from hotel parties. And that was the least of it.

Theodore found himself pushed aside as Lila, Cynthia and the other female mice worked feverishly on Lila's wedding dress and matching blue bridesmaid dresses for his six sisters.

On his off-duty hours, Theodore didn't know what to do with himself. He didn't even get much of a chance to talk to Lila.

Grandfather took him aside. "All this fuss is part of the normal routine. Just stay out of their way and show up for the ceremony. That's all you're required to do."

His mother found him sitting alone in their living room.

She sat down next to him and took his paw in hers. "I'm so happy for you, Theodore. I've talked to Lila, and she really, truly loves you."

He nodded, feeling a little bashful. "I love her too."

She smiled. "I know."

"Mother, Lila wants to see you right now," cried one of his sisters, running into the room.

Theodore's mother rose. "A wedding is for the bride. You just take it easy on your own."

Theodore nodded, wondering if Rocky Strong was in the same position.

He wandered up to the second floor and stood in the mice's area outside the ballroom. Peeking through a crack, he saw that a dance floor had already been set up in anticipation of the human reception.

There was no sign of Rocky. Theodore figured he'd probably been pushed aside too.

On the day of the wedding, while Lila and the bridal party took over his living quarters, Theodore went up to the second floor to check on Zanna and Rocky's wedding.

Music for their wedding could already be heard through the walls as the musicians warmed up. In no time, Rocky would be dancing with his bride.

"Yo! Having second thoughts?" asked Bandit, coming up beside him.

Theodore grinned and shook his head.

"Nice how things work out, huh?" said Bandit. "Glad you chose me to be your best man. And I promise to keep an eye on Zanna, now that she and my human will be together." He checked the shiny watch at his wrist. "C'mon, let's head down and get ready. It's time."

Theodore followed Bandit down to his room. He couldn't help feeling nervous. A week ago, he'd never met Lila. A suspected poisoning, then two had brought them together to save the hotel. What would the future hold for them?

Later, dressed in his best doorman uniform, Theodore, standing tall and proud, watched Lila glide down the aisle toward him. In place of her sparkly pink dress, Lila wore a long white gown that made her appear as if she were floating on a cloud. It all seemed a wonderful dream.

After the exchange of vows and a kiss that sent him reeling, he and Lila led everyone into the ballroom, which was decorated for the reception. The tables were covered with green tablecloths. Chairs were covered with blue fabric and tied with pink bows. Off to the side, a buffet table was filled with the best left-overs Theodore had ever seen. A mound of pieces of cake from the hotel formed a wedding cake of their own.

Theodore looked around with satisfaction. Everyone seemed to be having a wonderful time. He noticed Cynthia and Maurice laughing together. No doubt they'd be traveling together. He'd heard that Sam Horner's movie was a guaranteed success with Juliet taking a big role in it. They'd even added a wedding scene, featuring Zanna and Rocky. The only starlet missing was Simone. No one seemed to mind that she and that horrible dog of hers had flown home early.

Music from Zanna and Rocky's wedding flowed through the walls, sounding like a heart-felt melody to Theodore's ears. His adventures at The Winston Hotel had produced one love story after another. He smiled at Lila. Their love was the sweetest of all.

Bursting with happiness, Theodore gave Lila another twirl on the dance floor.

The Happy End

I hope you enjoyed Theodore and Lila's story in *WINNING BIG* and will let your friends know about them. I had a lot of fun writing this story. At the time, my husband and I were living in a hotel while he worked on a special project, and yes, there are some comparisons to life there!

Readers asked for more stories about The Hartwell Women, and I listened. Following is an excerpt from my book, *BABY TALK* (The Hartwell Women – 4).

CHAPTER ONE

On a clear, warm June day, I stood on the front porch of the house I now owned, staring out at the Maine coastline with a sigh of gratitude. I did this as often as I could. For me, taking a moment to appreciate all I'd been given had become a morning ritual I treasured.

In front of me, the blue-gray water met the sandy shore with a moist kiss, reared back like a shy lover—and then, tempted for more, embraced the shore again. Gulls cried out, swooped down, and lifted up in the air in unending musical acrobatics. A few large rocks, precursors of the rockier coastline down east, protruded from the water's surface like sea creatures wanting a peek at the world.

Almost two years ago, the sandy beach had hosted one of the most important events of my life. Even now, my pulse quickened at the memory of Brad saying "I do" and sweeping me into an embrace that drew applause. The simplicity of the ceremony had touched the hearts of everyone. What a wonderful day that had been. I still felt the thrill of belonging to his family and mine—the family I'd discovered after a lonely childhood. Thinking of the group gathered there, I thought how lucky I was and smiled up at the sun, letting its warmth wash over me.

The screen door opened and closed behind me. Brad stepped out onto the wide porch that swept the front of the seaside estate and wrapped his arms around me. "Good morning, Marissa Cole Crawford!" The sound of my married name on his lips still sent a tingle of delight throughout me.

I smiled and turned to him, inhaling the spicy aroma of his aftershave lotion. Snuggling into his strong embrace, I stared up at him, taking in the caramel-colored hair and toffee eyes that were his alone. I adored this man who'd given me so much love, so much confidence. I treasured our life together, so different from the background that had once been my life.

"You're off to Barnham?" I asked, hiding the loneliness I already felt at his upcoming departure.

He nodded. "Thank God this commuting back and forth will end in another year or so. I'm hoping Dad is fully retired by then, and we can finally sell the law practice to someone else." He gave me the lopsided grin I loved. "By then, we'll have started our family, and I can stay settled right here."

I didn't reply but rested my head against his firm chest. We'd been trying for a baby since the wedding. Brad was anxious to have children, but the thought scared me to death. I had so many doubts about myself as a mother. I'd been raised by one of the worst.

"Walk me out?" Brad slung his arm around my shoulder.

We headed through the elegant house I was slowly but surely trying to make into a real home—safe and welcoming to us both. Lady, my golden retriever, followed at our heels. She also hated to see Brad leave for his weekly trek to Barnham, New York.

Outside on the lawn, I gave Brad a lingering kiss, telling him in my own special way how much I'd miss him.

He pulled away and sighed. "See you on Friday. Have a good week. Love you, woman."

I smiled and played along with him. "Love you, man."

He laughed and climbed into his Jeep.

Watching him drive away, I wondered if I should confess my reluctance to have a baby. Each time another month went by without my getting pregnant, I was almost pleased about it ... until I saw his disappointment. But I was sure he'd be even more disappointed if I turned out to be anything like the cold, heartless mother with whom I'd grown up.

Moments later, Becky and Henry Cantwell drove down the driveway toward me, breaking into my disturbing thoughts. I waved and waited for them to park their truck by the garage and cross the lawn. They'd worked for my grandmother for years. I'd inherited them, along with the house I now miraculously owned. Watching them, I smiled with pleasure. They were so much more than a handyman and a housekeeper; they were the people who'd kept my dysfunctional family spiritually alive with their goodness.

"Brad gone already?" Becky asked.

"Didn't see his car," said Henry.

I nodded. "He'll be back on Friday."

"It'll be good when he can stay here permanently, don'tcha know," said Becky.

"And how," I quickly agreed. I looped my hand around Becky's arm, and we walked together toward the house as Henry headed back toward the garage. Becky and Doris, Brad's aunt, were two of the women I loved most in the world, along with my newfound cousins, Allison and Samantha Hartwell.

We entered the house, and I took a seat at the long, cherry

kitchen table to share a second cup of coffee with Becky. The kitchen was the heart of the house. It had been upgraded when the sunroom was added on to the house ten years ago. I'd left it pretty much the way it was when the house was given to me. The light cherry cupboards, some with etched glass doors, suited the formality of the green marble countertops. The Sub-Zero refrigerator, covered with cherry wood to match the cupboards, was unobtrusive among the cabinetry. But it was the six-burner Viking range that brought out the cook in me. It was Becky's pride and joy.

We finished our coffee, and when she went to work in the kitchen, I left her. When she was there, the kitchen was Becky's domain, which I respected. I stopped in the front hallway to freshen the flower arrangement and decided to take a look at the front of the house. Henry and I had talked about planting some flowers, and I wanted to see which of those he'd suggested would look best.

Lady went to the door and barked. I frowned. It wasn't like her.

I set aside the flower vase and went to the screen door, where I skidded to a stop. Gasping like a fish tossed out of water, I stared at a basket sitting on the floor of the porch by the door—a basket that held a baby. If the light pink blanket meant anything, it was a baby girl.

Heart pounding with alarm, I opened the door and dashed onto the porch. The baby stopped crying and stared at me. Yep, it was a baby, all right.

What?

I ran down the porch steps, searching for the person who might have left the little girl there. In the distance I could see a couple of joggers on the sand, two men. In the opposite direction, a young woman was running along the shore, long blond hair flying behind her like angel wings. I hurried out onto the lawn for a better look. Too far away to chase down or catch, I stared at the retreating figure.

Of course, maybe it wasn't her.

Turning in frantic circles, I surveyed the plantings around the house and the lawn beyond, but saw no sign of anyone lurking.

Pulse skipping, I raced back to the porch to the baby who was now crying. Staring at her red face, and her flailing arms, shock roared through me. *Oh my God! What am I going to do?*

Becky appeared in the doorway. "My stars! What's this?"

"A baby," I said. Panic sent my voice to a higher register. "Someone left a baby here. We have to find the mother!"

Becky stepped out onto the porch and lifted the crying baby out of the basket. As she did, a note fell to the floor below. I snatched it up. "Dear Mrs. Crawford, I've watched you and your husband for a while now. Seeing as you have no kids of your own, I thought this would be a perfect place for Summer Marie to live. Take care of her because I can't. Please, please don't put her in the foster care system. I know it too well."

I rocked back on my heels. My heart beat so fast, I felt faint. This had to be a joke. Things like this didn't really happen, did they? I stared once more at the note, but the words did a dance on the page that blurred my vision. I looked to Becky. "What are we going to do?" I felt sick to my stomach.

Becky cooed softly to the baby and checked her over. Thin strands of light brown hair spread atop the baby's head. Her eyes, a navy blue, were alert as she tried to focus. Dressed in pale-green pajamas, she kicked her feet and howled, turning her fine-featured face a bright red.

"She's a beautiful little girl," said Becky, "but she's hungry and wet. I'll send Henry down to the store for supplies. Then we'll figure this out."

Before I could protest, Becky wrapped the pink blanket around the baby and placed her in my arms. "Here. You take her while I make a list for Henry."

The baby stopped crying and studied me solemnly, no doubt wondering what had happened to land her in a stranger's arms.

Becky nodded with satisfaction at the quietness. "See? That's a sign." She walked away, leaving me alone with the baby.

A sign of what? Feeling numb from all that'd happened and what it might mean, I paced the front porch with the baby. She started to cry again. Crazy thoughts circled around in my mind like the whirling wind in a summer storm. Surely, no one thought I should keep this abandoned child. Or was this some kind of fate thing to test me as a person? Or worse yet, was it someone's nasty joke?

The baby made a face, and it suddenly became quite clear she needed a new diaper. I gagged at the smell, and gasping with dismay at the mess, I called for Becky.

"Oh, my goodness!" Becky said when she saw what had happened. "It just might be time for a little bath for Summer Marie. Come along, Marissa. You can help me get her cleaned up."

I held the baby away from me while Becky ran a shallow amount of warm water in the kitchen sink and laid a soft towel on the bottom. She took the baby and removed the soiled clothes from her little body. "Ahhh, she's a beautiful little girl, just perfect," she murmured, setting her down carefully into the water. "Who would give up a darling baby like this?"

"Her mother said she couldn't take care of her." Gazing at

the baby I was now supposed to take care of, I clasped my hands together helplessly. "How old do you think she is?"

The little girl cooed and kicked her feet in the water. Drops of water splashed around her like sparkling diamonds.

Becky gently washed the baby's body with the mild soap she kept at the sink for herself. "Can't be absolutely sure, but I'm guessing she's just a couple months old. She's a young one all right," she said.

After rinsing her, she drained the water, patted the clean baby dry, and wrapped her up in a soft towel.

She seemed so competent to me.

"That'll hold her until Henry returns." Becky chuckled softly. "When I told him what was up, he flew out of here like a rabbit on the run."

I smiled. Henry was one big softie wrapped in a brusque Maine manner. My smile evaporated. "I'd better call Brad. I know there are some legal issues here."

Becky nodded. "I think we should take the baby to Dr. Storey and have him check her out before any authorities are called. The mother didn't want the baby in the system. I don't much care for that idea myself."

I nodded and punched in the numbers for Brad's cell. As I recited the news to him, I couldn't help the tears that stung my eyes. My emotions were on a merry-go-round of self-doubt and concern for the baby.

Brad listened to me, then he spoke calmly. "The authorities will have to be notified, but my understanding of the law indicates Becky is right. You can place her with Dr. Storey, who would be considered a safe haven provider. He would then have to make the proper notification to the Department of Children and Families. He might even be willing to press upon the authorities the need for an immediate placement and ask for you to be made the temporary custodian of the child."

Hearing the cold, professional words, my heart sank. The mother, whoever she was, didn't want the baby placed in the system, but I wasn't sure I wanted to take on the responsibility of this child either, even for a short time.

Henry returned from the store loaded down with diapers, all the fixings for bottle-feeding, clothes, blankets, lotions, and even a small pink stuffed lamb. When he saw the baby, his features softened. He approached Summer on tiptoes.

Becky pulled the towel away from Summer's face so Henry could see.

"Sure is a little mite," Henry said. "A pretty one at that." He turned to me. "You gonna keep her?"

"I'm hoping to find the baby's mother. Her mother must have loved her. The note said she'd been watching Brad and me for some time before choosing us to take her." Not for the first time, the thought of being spied upon sent a shiver dancing across my shoulders.

"We're taking it one step at a time," Becky said briskly. "We'll get her dressed and fed, and then we're taking her to see Dr. Storey. From there, who knows. But I, for one, don't want to see the authorities take her away, don'tcha know." There was a maternal warning in Becky's tone I envied.

I left Becky and Henry in the kitchen and walked out onto the porch. Placing the basket on the white wooden railing, I lifted out the small mattress, searching for clues. But the plain white mattress cover told me nothing, and the empty basket was generic. My thoughts flew to the girl running down the beach. Was she the mother? If so, finding her would be like finding a needle in a haystack. There were at least three dozen young girls with long, blond-streaked hair in New Hope alone. During the summer, even more.

###

Dr. Storey was a short, stocky man who, with his shaggy brown hair, button dark eyes, and wide smile, reminded me of a friendly teddy bear. Watching him gently examine Summer, I was glad we'd brought her to him first.

"She's a fine, healthy baby girl," he said, handing the baby to me.

"Have you seen her before? We're trying to find the mother," I said.

He shook his head. "She's not been a patient of mine." He studied me a moment. "Your husband called me. In light of the note the mother left you, he's thinking the baby should be placed with you until her situation is settled. How do you feel about that?"

I gulped, wondering if I should be honest and tell him the baby might be better off with someone else.

"That's a very good idea, Dr. Storey," Becky said before I could respond. "We'll see to it that she has the best of care. Won't we, Marissa?"

I nodded. With Becky's help, maybe I could do it. But that didn't mean I'd stop looking for the baby's mother. Something must be terribly wrong for a mother to give up a beautiful child like this, especially when she cared enough to make sure her baby was placed in a nice home.

About the Author

Judith Keim was born and raised in Elmira, New York, and now makes her home in Idaho with her husband, her long-haired dachshund, Winston, and other members of her family.

"Growing up, books were always present—being read, ready to go back to the library, or about to be discovered. Information from the books was shared in general conversation, giving all of us in the family a wealth of knowledge and a lot of imagination. Perhaps that is why I was drawn to the idea of writing stories early on. I particularly love to write novels about women who deal with the unexpected with strength and open their hearts to finding love, because no matter what our circumstances, we all need to love and be loved in return.

"I hope you've enjoyed this book. If you have, please help other readers discover it by leaving a review on Amazon, Goodreads, or the site of your choice. And please check out the Hartwell Women Series, the Fat Fridays Group, and the other Beach House Hotel books. ALL THE BOOKS ARE NOW AVAILABLE IN AUDIO! So fun to have these characters come alive!"

Ms. Keim can be reached at www.judithkeim.com And to like her author page on Facebook and keep up with the news, go to:
https://www.facebook.com/pages/Judith-Keim/184013771644484?ref=aymt_homepage_panel

To receive notices about new books, follow her on Book Bub - http://bit.ly/2pZBDXq

And here's a link to where you can sign up for her periodic newsletter!
http://eepurl.com/bZoICX

She is also on twitter: @judithkeim, LinkedIn and Goodreads.

BOOKS BY JUDITH KEIM

The Talking Tree (The Hartwell Women –1)
Sweet Talk (The Hartwell Women – 2)
Straight Talk (The Hartwell Women – 3)
Baby Talk (The Hartwell Women – 4)
The Hartwell Women Series – (Boxed Set)
Breakfast at The Beach House Hotel –1
Lunch at The Beach House Hotel – 2
Dinner at The Beach House Hotel – 3
Christmas at The Beach House Hotel – 4
Fat Fridays (Fat Fridays Group – 1)
Sassy Saturdays (Fat Fridays Group – 2)
Secret Sundays (Fat Fridays Group – 3 – (Coming soon!)
Finding Me – A Salty Key Inn Book – 1
Finding My Way – A Salty Key Inn Book – 2)
Finding Love – A Salty Key Inn Book – 3 (Winter 2018)
Finding Family – A Salty Key Inn Book – 4 (Autumn 2018)
Winning BIG – a little love story for all ages
For more information: http://amzn.to/2jamIaF

CHILDREN'S BOOKS BY J. S. KEIM

The Hidden Moon (The Hidden Moon Series – 1)
Return to the Hidden Moon (The Hidden Moon Series – 2)
Trouble on the Hidden Moon (The Hidden Moon Series – 3)
Kermit Greene's World
For more information: http://amzn.to/2qlqKMI

83263807R00068

Made in the USA
Lexington, KY
10 March 2018